Jack grinned, things to Kell

"So I have a cook?" he said.

"You have a cook."

His blue-black eyes held hers for several long, nerve-tingling seconds before he took out his notepad, jotted down a telephone number and handed her the slip of paper.

"You can reach me on that number. Think carefully about what you're getting yourself into, Kelly." He added crisply, "You've got a week to change your mind!"

Rosemary Badger was born in Canada. At school she had a teacher who read to the class every day. Her reading was sheer magic. If the story was sad, the whole class sobbed. If it was funny, everyone roared. Rosemary had always loved reading but this teacher made her yearn to write! Rosemary now lives with her husband and four children in the beautiful town of Bundaberg, in Queensland, Australia, surrounded by glorious beaches and savouring the warm subtropical climate.

THE
HERO TRAP

BY
ROSEMARY BADGER

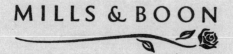

FOR JANET ELIZABETH GARLICK (née Keeler)
A Treasured Friend.

*MILLS & BOON and the Rose Device
are trademarks of the publisher.
Harlequin Mills & Boon Limited,
Eton House, 18-24 Paradise Road, Richmond, Surrey, TW9 1SR*

© Rosemary Badger 1995

ISBN 0 263 79384 2

*Set in Times Roman 10 on 12pt
01-9602-56330 C1*

Made and printed in Great Britain

CHAPTER ONE

DAMN that Jack Saunders!

Kelly McGuire walked slowly along the windswept
beach at Bargara, on Australia's subtropical Queensland
coast, silently cursing the man who had destroyed her
business. Her head was bent into the wind and her hands
were shoved into the pockets of her jeans. A bright yellow
scarf, tied into a bow at the back of her neck and the
same colour as her jumper, did its best to keep her thick
mane of auburn hair from becoming hopelessly tangled
in the howling spring gale.

A worried frown marred her smooth brow and she
dug her teeth deeper into her bottom lip. Her small
savings were almost gone. Unless some jobs came her
way, and soon, she would be forced out of the old beach
shack she had been lucky enough to rent. The run-down
shack, hardly more than a hut, was even owned by the
man.

She stopped in front of the tiny shack. It could barely
be seen through the gnarled mass of overgrown shrubs
and spindly trees that had been allowed to grow around
it unattended over the years. Beside it, but clearly visible,
were twenty-four brand-new town houses. The elegant
town houses, set in their magnificent landscaped gardens,
served as a constant reminder of what the enormously
wealthy and powerful business tycoon had done to her.

And she had helped him do it! That was the worst
part. If only she hadn't been so sure of herself then

perhaps she wouldn't have presented such an easy target for Saunders. If only she hadn't decided she was some sort of knight in shining armour sent to defend the small and weak against the big and powerful. Kelly sighed heavily and started up the path towards the shack. If only she had kept her mouth shut!

It had all started so innocently. A chance of a lifetime, or so she had thought, when Saunders called in tenders for the landscaping of his stately town houses. Being connected with a project of this grandeur was just what her fledgling business needed to establish a reputation for being, well, not just a good landscape gardener but a great one. Submitting a tender and hopeful of winning a small part of the project, Kelly had carefully selected and purchased some much needed second-hand equipment, lined up a young labourer and nervously kept her fingers crossed.

The lucrative job was given to a huge landscaping firm in Brisbane! None of the locals had even been considered. She had felt so cheated. So had all the others. But Kelly was the only one to protest and she did so at every opportunity, on the streets, over the radio and through letters to the editor of the local newspaper. She became something of a celebrity, much admired for daring to take a stand against 'powerful outside investors like Jack Saunders who exploited the locals, dried them up, froze them out by using huge, outside conglomerates.'

The publicity brought an unexpected windfall. Jobs! Lots of them. It seemed everyone wanted the local heroine to put in or tend to their gardens. Kelly put on the labourer she had lined up and hired another to keep up with the demand. At the age of twenty-six and after a long, hard struggle of putting herself through university, working and skimping and finally saving up enough to launch her own business, life was starting to look pretty darn good.

The good life ended abruptly. It ended when she accepted an invitation to tape a television segment for the six o'clock news. The interview was to take place at Saunders's controversial site.

'If only I had said no,' Kelly muttered aloud as she continued along the winding path towards the shack. 'If only I hadn't been so eager to sink a few more barbs into Jack Saunders's miserable hide!'

The interview was scheduled for two o'clock. Kelly left her two young employees to carry on with the rock garden they were installing for an elderly couple, wiped her hands on an old rag, coaxed a few damp strands of auburn hair under her wide-brimmed straw hat, tucked her blue cotton T-shirt into the waistband of her jeans, hopped into her old utility and sped jubilantly off to the site.

The television crew, consisting of an attractive young journalist and a boyish-looking cameraman, weren't the only ones waiting for her! A tall, rugged giant of a man, dressed in a dark blue business suit was with them. His suit was expertly tailored, obviously expensive, the soft material hugging his broad shoulders and the long, straight columns of his legs. His shirt was a crisp white, the collar brilliant against his deep tan. A silk tie in contrasting shades of blue completed the picture of a very impressive man. Kelly had only seen him from a distance and had never spoken to him, but she knew immediately who this man was. *Jack Saunders*! Well, she certainly welcomed the opportunity to finally say to his face what she had been saying on the streets, the news-paper and the radio.

The utility ground to a halt close to where they were standing, Saunders in front, obviously in charge. A bit of gravel from the vehicle's wheels shot up and sprayed his trousered legs. He peered down in annoyance. Kelly whisked off her straw hat, ran her slender fingers through the glorious tangled mass of her hair, stepped from the ute and smiled boldly up at him.

Up close he was younger than she had thought him to be, probably just into his thirties. His hair was jet black, straight, parted on the side, thick and vibrantly glossy, totally free of any dressings to keep it in place. His forehead was wide, intelligent, and his hair fell over it almost touching his equally black brows above the deepest, darkest, bluest eyes imaginable. There was a healthy glow to his tanned skin and his mouth was wide, perfectly sculptured, hinting at a deep sensuality and not just a little cruelty. He exuded a power and strength that was almost frightening.

'So *you* are Kelly McGuire!' he growled, making her name sound like a notorious bush-ranger's or worse! Kelly proudly drew herself up to her full height of five feet seven inches.

'And *you* must be Jack Saunders,' she hissed, deli-berately making his name sound like a collection of ven-omous snakes! His deep blue eyes narrowed shrewdly on her face and she immediately felt a burning heat scorch her cheeks. *Don't let him unsettle you*! she quickly warned herself.

But when those same blue eyes drifted slowly over her, from the top of her brilliant auburn hair tumbling with a wild abandonment down to her slender shoulders, to linger slightly longer on the small, uptilted breasts beneath the thin fabric of her cotton T-shirt before casually taking in her trim waist, long, slender, jean-clad legs, and feet encased in brown work boots, Kelly knew she was losing the battle.

And when the seductive journey was mercilessly repeated, with those cobalt blue orbs drifting leisurely up again to the strawberry moistness of her trembling lips to settle with a keen shrewdness on the green lights glittering angrily in her eyes, Kelly knew she had very little armour against this man. She stood helplessly in front of him, detesting his blatant appraisal of her, detesting those arresting blue eyes holding her captive, detesting *herself* for letting him get away with it, for not giving him a swift kick in the shin with the steel toe of her work boot!

Saunders continued to take charge. He stated that the interview would take place, not on the roadside facing the complex as suggested by the journalist, but rather where the *landscaping*, the reason for them being here, he had added pointedly looking straight into Kelly's eyes, was in full progress. Leading the way, he cast aside his domineering manner and became instantly charming.

Too charming! Kelly decided suspiciously. She followed in the rear, disgusted that the journalist and cameraman could be so easily wooed by Saunders's deep baritone voice and brilliant white smile as he boastfully listed the many virtues of his fabulous complex. Sickening! she thought. It's not *that* magnificent but she knew that it was.

The fresh clean odours of mortar, plaster and paint assailed their nostrils as they followed a boarded path between the stately town houses, each one uniquely different with its own distinctive personality. Kelly knew them well. She had spent days, weeks, designing perfect little gardens for each one of them.

Saunders brought the trio to a halt at the edge of a clump of casuarina trees, their long, silvery needles bending in the soft sea breezes. Behind them was a fleet of impressive white vans with the words SUPERIOR LANDSCAPE ARCHITECTS boldly emblazoned along their sides. Kelly's mouth dropped open in dismay. Landscape *Architects*? Good grief! Well, she hoped they were charging him a fortune.

The cameraman immediately shifted the camera onto his shoulder and zoomed over the complex. Saunders nodded his approval and after a few minutes signalled to the journalist. She cleared her throat and obediently faced the camera.

'There has been much controversy over the landscaping of this fabulous beachfront housing complex here at Bargara. The lucrative job was given to an outside firm of landscape architects. With me is the Brisbane owner and builder of these luxury dwellings, Mr Jack Saunders, and local gardener, Miss Kelly McGuire, who had led the campaign against Mr. Saunders. Miss McGuire has publicly voiced keen disapproval at being one of the many local tradespeople snubbed by Jack Saunders.' She smiled prettily at Saunders and cooed, 'Why did you overlook our local tradespeople, Mr Saunders?'

Kelly's mouth tightened and her heart pounded as she relived the rest of the interview. Jack Saunders started off praising the submissions he had received. His voice was charged with sincerity while he told how some of the tenders had come close to being awarded the lucrative contract.

'The only thing holding them back,' he had insisted, 'was their lack of experience and equipment for a job of this vastness, this scale, this enormity.' He turned and smiled tolerantly down at Kelly. 'Miss McGuire totally misunderstood what was involved here. Miss McGuire,' he sighed, giving the impression he considered her somewhat dim, 'seemed to think a seeded lawn, a few trees, shrubs and flowers was all that was needed.' The journalist and cameraman grinned. Kelly's cheeks turned crimson.

'I didn't think that at all,' she quickly insisted and immediately realised that by the sudden lifting of his arrogant brows she had somehow played straight into his hands.

'Didn't *think*, Miss McGuire? Didn't *think* about drainage systems? Or lighting systems?'

'Well, no, I mean, yes, yes of course I did, but I wasn't—'

'What about filtering systems?' he interrupted harshly. 'Did you spare a thought for them? Or sprinkling systems? What about picnic and play areas, creating passageways with the proper coatings and underlays? And what about swimming pools, wading pools, tennis and squash courts, Miss McGuire? You completely left them out of your submission.'

He had waited patiently then, giving her a chance to speak. But she could only gaze helplessly up at him, too choked by humiliation to utter a single word.

'Well! Well! Well!' he had drawled softly. 'Suddenly you have *nothing* to say?' He reached into his breast coat pocket and withdrew a large envelope. It was the submission she had laboured over.

'I guess this says it all, doesn't it, Miss McGuire? You're a gardener, and judging from this submission, a pretty good one with plenty of imagination and flare.' His voice hardened. 'But you are *not* a landscape architect capable of undertaking the *whole* of this project, start to finish, which is what the tender called for. This is a multimillion-dollar complex, Miss McGuire. There's no room for amateurs!'

He gently pressed the submission into her trembling hand, firmly wrapped her frozen fingers around it, a final convincing gesture to show how wrongly he had been accused and how unjustifiably provoked! The pretty journalist said as much as she wrapped up the interview, warmly thanked Saunders for his time, coldly thanked Kelly for hers. The camera rolled to a halt. The interview was over but the nightmare had barely begun!

Pleased with his success, and obviously not one to miss an opportunity, Saunders had chatted amicably with the crew while leading them towards the nearest town house. With the camera rolling once again, he opened the door and ushered them inside. Kelly could hardly believe the gall, the nerve, the sheer audacity of this man. Thanks to her, his multimillion-dollar complex was receiving a fortune in free advertising. Thanks to him, she would probably become the laughing-stock of the town.

Humiliated and disheartened, Kelly made her way slowly back along the boarded path towards the utility. He hadn't given her a chance to speak, to explain how she and several of the other tradespeople had innocently assumed he would use subcontractors for various sections of his huge project. Surely people would see that and not like him for it. But even as she thought this, Kelly knew it wouldn't happen that way. He had charmed the journalist and cameraman and he would charm the viewing audience.

She reached the utility and opened the door. Strong, warm hands gripped her shoulders, spun her around. And there they were again, those lightning blue eyes.

'Let go of me!' Kelly gasped and struggled to free herself. Jack merely tightened his grip on her slender shoulders. 'Didn't you hear me?' she shrieked. 'I said let go of me, damn you!'

'I will. In a moment. After we chat.'

'*Chat*?' She couldn't believe her ears. '*Chat*!' Her green eyes blazed up at him. 'How dare you suggest we chat after what you did to me back there?'

He shrugged his huge shoulders. 'I did what had to be done. What you deserved!'

'You *crucified* me!'

'You were becoming a nuisance.'

'A nuisance! By standing up for myself and others? By wanting a fair go?'

'A "fair go" is a two-way street, Kelly McGuire.' His voice matched the hardness in his eyes. 'You might have brought your grievances to me instead of howling to the media.'

'I might have, had I thought it would do any good.' She added in disgust, 'You big land developers are all alike. You take and take and take and never give anything back!'

An angry flush stormed across his hard cheeks. 'It seems you make a practice of making wild statements, Miss McGuire,' he stated harshly. 'As it happens, most materials used in constructing my town houses were purchased locally. I've hired local tradespeople wherever possible and my own construction crews, engineers and architects have rented homes, flats or stayed in motels during their time here. They've purchased groceries, clothes, petrol, gifts for their families and spent money on movies and other entertainment. Add to that the very considerable sums spent on council fees, land tax, sales tax, rates and road improvement and I think you must agree, Miss McGuire, that on the whole, this town has fared rather nicely under us. Rather nicely indeed,' he added arrogantly, his look telling her he fully expected an apology.

But Kelly was in no mood to apologise. A lot of people might have benefited but she hadn't been one of them, nor had any of her colleagues. True, her protests had brought her work but that had been a by-product of her own undertaking, she quickly reminded herself.

'What a pity your benevolence stopped short at gardening!' she muttered and shot him a withering glare.

So! he thought. There was to be no apology! His fingers twitched on her shoulders as he resisted the urge to shake her.

'What a pity indeed!' he drawled and his hands moved slowly down her slender arms sending her pulses racing and her anger soaring.

Kelly struggled in vain to free herself but his fingers were like bands of steel encircling her wrists. He pulled her abruptly up to his chest and she tingled at the unexpected contact. Fury danced in her eyes making them seem even more beautiful. He bent his head as if to kiss her. Kelly's heart pounded in her chest.

'Forget about any further grandstanding, Kelly,' he stated softly and released her. 'Get on with your own business and leave others to theirs!'

An indignant flush rose high on her cheeks. 'Are you threatening me, Jack Saunders? Because if you are, I'll have you know that—' Her words ended in a startled gasp when he raised his hand and ran a finger lightly across her trembling lips, effectively silencing her.

'There, that's better!' His sudden grin revealed a set of handsome male dimples. 'Do you know what I think would be a damned good idea?' he added cheerfully.

'For you to leave town?' she muttered hatefully.

'No, no, nothing like that.' He cupped her chin in his huge hand and forced her to look up at him. 'We could watch the interview together!' The grin romped straight into his wicked blue eyes. 'How about it, McGuire? Your place or mine? We could even make a night of it,' he continued suggestively. 'Well, what do you say?'

'*Go jump in the lake*!'

Kelly climbed stiffly into the cab of her utility and sped off, the churning wheels showering Saunders once more with gravel. But he hardly seemed to notice, much less care. The grin slowly widened as he loosened the blue silk tie at his neck, undid the top button of his crisp white shirt and shoved his hands into the pockets of his trousers. He watched her roar down the road and tried to remember the last time he had felt this alive, this great!

Kelly watched him through her rear-view mirror, saw him loosen his tie, undo the button, shove his hands into his pockets. She felt sure he was humming or whistling or *something*! He deserved to be shot! The wheels of the utility screamed in protest as she swiftly took a bend, anxious to be out of his sight.

But she couldn't relax. Her knuckles were white on the steering wheel, her jaw tightly clenched, her back stiff. When she finished work that evening she didn't do what she always did after a hard day toiling under the hot sun. She didn't strip and enjoy a long, refreshingly cool shower before preparing a light meal and having it on the balcony of her small, two-bedroom apartment overlooking the sea. Instead, she headed straight for the living room and stood in front of the television set, staring warily down at the empty screen. It was almost six o'clock, time for the news. She bent forward and pressed the switch.

Various items ranging from the plight of the district's sugar-cane farmers struggling with the fall of world prices, to the increasing vandalism in the neighbouring town of Bundaberg's central business area, danced across the screen. As the stories gradually unfolded, Kelly felt herself daring to relax. The local news was almost over. Perhaps they had axed her interview with Jack Saunders. But far from axing it, they had simply saved it for the last, a dramatic finale to the day's events.

She looked like a teenage delinquent dressed as she was in her blue jeans, T-shirt and work boots compared to Jack Saunders's impeccable elegance and that of the attractive journalist. Her flamboyant auburn hair had never looked so wild, the wind tossing it about her face but not quite managing to hide, first the smug confidence, then the blazing defiance, and finally the humiliation as she glared up at Saunders. The camera showed her no mercy, zooming in on her hands nervously twisting the brim of her old straw hat as she struggled unsuccessfully to answer his simple questions.

Jack Saunders had made her look like a fool, even worse, a troublemaker.

The ones who had encouraged her the most were the first to turn against her. She was bailed up on the street and accused of trying to turn 'big business' away. It seemed everyone had suddenly realised just how much their tiny hamlet had profited from Jack Saunders's presence in their tiny community. Over the next few days all the jobs she had lined up were cancelled and no others were forthcoming. She held out as long as she could but was finally forced to let her employees go and rent out her precious apartment to help cover the mortgage payments. It was the first real home she had known since orphaned at ten and shunted from relative to relative. Now the dilapidated old shack, with its paint peeling from the walls, seemed to reflect her despair as she climbed the creaking steps leading up to the rickety veranda.

The sound of a car's powerful engine purring to a halt, followed immediately by a door slamming shut, caused Kelly to halt on the steps. She stiffened, head raised high, beautiful green eyes narrowed, wary, every muscle in her body tensed, ready for flight, ready to seek refuge.

For this was what she always did whenever she heard the unmistakable sound of Jack Saunders's sleek grey Jaguar convertible pulling into the driveway backing onto his fabulous complex. If she was too far from the shack to reach it safely without being detected, she quickly took refuge behind whatever was available: a tree, a boulder, a depression in the sand-dunes. Not only couldn't she bear the sight of the man but she refused to allow him the satisfaction of seeing what he had done to her, how his actions had forced her to live like a destitute hermit in his run-down, overgrown shack, right next to the exquisite, parklike setting he had used to destroy her.

Usually, she didn't have to hide long. Saunders mainly made lightning-swift stops to check on the landscape architects before rushing off again. But the final touches to the landscaping had been completed yesterday so she really had no idea how much time he would spend admiring the finished product!

She heard his firm footsteps on one of the tile walkways closest to the shack. But this time, instead of running inside, Kelly swallowed her pride and didn't move. Her small savings were gone, the rent was due and a girl had to eat. She could no longer afford to hide from him.

Kelly could see him clearly now, and even though she detested him, she couldn't help but be affected by his devastating good looks. He wasn't wearing one of his exquisite tailor-made business suits but was dressed instead in a pair of blue jeans topped with a black woollen sweater, the sleeves pushed up his tanned forearms, and on his feet were a pair of brown leather sports shoes. The wind tossed his thick glossy black hair away from his forehead and deepened his ruddy complexion. He looked more like an incredibly fit athlete than the heartless entrepreneur she knew him to be.

She walked slowly towards the edge of the veranda, and with her heart thumping in her chest, stood there, hoping he would notice and call out to her. It seemed important, somehow, that it should happen this way.

CHAPTER TWO

JACK knew Kelly was there, standing on the veranda of
the old shack. He had seen her the moment he had
stepped onto the path leading into the gardens. Smiling
to himself, he decided to ignore her, and instead began
a brisk stroll around the gardens, making his final inspection of the landscaping.

Now that the landscaping was completed he had put
the town houses on the market. Twelve had been sold
straight off the plans, and with the enormous public
interest his complex had received, he knew there wouldn't
be any difficulty selling the remainder. Offers were
pouring in.

His profit would be enormous. Beachfront land up
here at Bargara, only a short drive from Bundaberg,
home of the world-famous rum, was ridiculously cheap
compared to down south. And he had been smart enough
to purchase several hundred hectares along the north-
eastern coast years ago when prices were cheaper still.
When the massive wealth of the Gold and Sunshine
coasts flowed north he would greet the big global
investors at his very own beachfront doors! All part of
a plan. The town houses were simply a start, a hint of
what was to come. By the time he had utilised all his
land, here and at the Whitsunday Islands on the Great
Barrier Reef where he had already commenced work on
his island resort, there would be several more complexes
even more magnificent than this.

Like most shrewd businessmen, Jack felt no particular pride in his achievements. Luck played no part in any of his dealings. His brilliance, his lack of fear, his uncanny insight into knowing instinctively what would work and what wouldn't had spiralled him to the top of the business world. Now at the age of thirty-four this tough young entrepreneur was a millionaire many times over with business interests spanning the globe, ranging from gold and timber, to concrete and steel.

Kelly's eyes remained rigidly fixed on the tall, dark figure of the man she loathed. She saw him stop abruptly to closely examine a young sapling. A frown swept across his ruggedly handsome face. The glowering frown deepened as he jotted something down on a small notepad retrieved from the back pocket of his jeans. *So all was not well with his fancy landscaping*!

She held her breath each time Saunders stopped to closely examine a bed of flowers, a row of shrubs or a line of trees, eagerly awaiting the notepad to be whipped out, the black frown to appear, some dreadful complaint jotted down. When he had finally completed his thorough inspection and still hadn't noticed her, Kelly realised she would need to make the first move. With the landscaping completed, he would most likely be heading straight back to Brisbane and she might never see him again.

Taking a deep, steadying breath, Kelly stepped from the veranda and onto the sand making her way slowly towards him. He stood now with his powerful shoulders slightly hunched into the wind, hands shoved into the pockets of his jeans, a dark, brooding expression on his face as he gazed silently out to sea.

She stood awkwardly apart from him and a little to his side, reluctant to disturb him. The invigorating breeze howled in from the ocean, finally freeing her tangled, wind-blown hair from its yellow scarf and sweeping his own raven black hair away from his brow. The scarf fluttered playfully in the wind before dropping suddenly to the lush, green, manicured lawn, to rest dangerously close to his brown leather sports shoes. Kelly held her breath, not daring to retrieve it, while wondering if he knew it was there... or even that she was!

Her eyes were drawn to his profile as he continued his silent gaze out to sea. Even though he was devastatingly handsome, there was certainly nothing soft or feminine about his features. Indeed, there was a hardness about him, a firmness, a great strength that couldn't be denied or ignored. And hadn't she already experienced these formidable qualities along with a sample of his heart-lessness? Kelly quickly reminded herself, shocked that his good looks were again distracting her.

Jack bent down, picked up the scarf, turned and held it out to her. Kelly hesitated for several seconds before slowly reaching for it, her trembling fingers brushing against his as she accepted it. The brief contact was enough to send a shiver of shock all the way up her arm.

'Thank you,' she whispered hoarsely and, avoiding his eyes, busied herself with the task of tucking the scarf into the pocket of her jeans.

'I'm surprised to see you,' he said and the mysterious tone of his voice caused her to look up quickly. Her already-rosy cheeks flooded with fresh colour when she saw the glitter of amusement in his eyes. Her colour deepened even more when he added softly, 'Usually you go to such extravagant lengths to ensure that I don't!'

'What...what do you mean?' she asked hesitantly, her throat suddenly dry. He had obviously witnessed her many frantic attempts to hide from him! She might have realised a man like Jack Saunders would have eyes in the back of his head! Of course he would. Her contempt for him soared. 'I...I wasn't...wasn't *hiding* from you if that's what you're suggesting,' she added indignantly.

'No?'

Her flush deepened. 'No.'

'What *were* you doing then?'

'Well, I was...I was simply...'

'Avoiding me?' he suggested and her tell-tale flush gave him his answer. He chuckled softly and raised his black, arrogant brows. 'Avoiding me by moving into my beach house, only metres from my complex?' He placed his hands on her shoulders and pulled her against the hard rock wall of his chest. His full dark mouth was mere centimetres from hers, hovering above her trembling lips. Her startled green eyes were wide and unblinking as she stared into the glittering blue depths of his own. For several seconds they stayed like that, not moving, simply looking into each other's eyes, searching for answers to unspoken questions.

'The truth, Kelly McGuire!' he growled softly, his hands firm but amazingly gentle on the slender curves of her shoulders. 'Why did you move into my beach shack?'

Kelly swallowed hard. Now was the time to tell him, tell him what their interview had done to her, what it had cost. Now was the time to do what she had come to do. To throw herself at his mercy and beg for his help, beg for a job, any job! But when she opened her mouth to speak, the words simply refused to come.

Perhaps it was the way he was looking at her. Was it pity or concern she saw etched in those deep blue eyes? She couldn't be sure. But if it was pity, she would rather starve to death than have him feast off it. Salvaging what was left of her pride, Kelly shook her head and then to her horror felt tears searing the backs of her eyes. She broke from his grip, turned and walked quickly away, desperate to get as far away as possible before the wretched things betrayed her.

'*Kelly*! *Stop*!'

His deep voice was so commanding she actually hesitated as if to obey before quickening her pace.

'*Kelly*!'

This time she broke into a run. She ran through the fringe of trees separating his two properties, across the shifting sands and clumps of dried yellow grasses to the steps leading up to the shack. She flung open the door, stumbled inside, slammed it shut behind her. The key flew out of the lock and onto the wooden floor. She fell to her knees, frantically searching for it in the gloom of the semi-darkness. Her heart stopped, then skittered across her chest when she heard his firm steps on the veranda, the creak of the ageing boards under his weight.

The door opened and he stood there, a tall giant of a man silhouetted against the twilight of the late afternoon. His deep blue eyes narrowed instantly on her flushed face as she crouched on the floor, the key held tightly in her trembling hand revealing her intention. He smiled grimly, stepped across the threshold, shut the door behind him, reached for her hand, helped her up, removed the key, returned it to the lock, and took a swift glance around the tiny shack.

He hadn't been inside the place for years, not since he had inherited it along with the vast acreage he had purchased. The blinds were yellowed with time, tattered, sprinkled with holes. The wooden floorboards were bare of any carpeting, the slab walls of any ornament. In a corner beside the door squatted an ancient lounge chair, the bulging cushion covered with a clean white bath towel, another covering the back. At the opposite end of the room was a chipped sink boasting a single tap. A bright red Esky sat on a counter next to the sink, obviously serving as a fridge. A small table and chair completed the kitchen and dining area. There was nothing else, no other furniture, no other conveniences, certainly no luxuries.

Off this small room was another of equal size. The door was open. An ageing blind covered the single window. A mattress was made up on the floor. Next to it was an orderly stack of what appeared to be gardening magazines. Clothing was arranged neatly on a row of hooks. The inspection had taken mere seconds but it was enough for Kelly to regain her composure. She stood in front of the window and the last rays of the afternoon sun pierced through the holes of the blind, capturing her flamboyant hair and transforming it into raging streams of liquid flame. Jack's eyes rested on the sheer beauty of it and he wondered what it would feel like in his hands, what it would look like slipping between his fingers.

'Why did you run away?' His voice was a deep rumble in the stillness of the tiny room.

'Why did you follow me?' Her voice sounded small against the timbre of his own.

'My question first.'

She shrugged her slender shoulders. 'I didn't run away. I . . . I was cold. I wanted to get h-home.'

'Home?' He shook his dark head and watched her closely. 'This isn't home. Home is a very attractive beachfront apartment on the foreshore.'

Kelly's eyes widened. 'How did you know?'

'Does it matter?'

'Yes.'

'It wasn't hard in a town this size.' He had the cheek to add, 'Besides, everyone knows where Kelly McGuire lives!'

'Used to live,' Kelly stiffly corrected him. 'Now, I live...' She glanced quickly around at the drab little hut. 'Now I live here.'

Jack followed her glance. 'I must admit I was rather surprised when the real-estate agent asked if I would lease the place. At first I said no but when I learned it was yourself who was so desperate to have it, I thought, hey, what the heck, for old times' sake, why not?'

'Why not indeed!' Kelly repeated tersely and resisted the urge to strike him, to lash out at him, to do anything that might effectively remove that irritating expression of smug arrogance from his handsome face. Instead, she added sweetly, 'What surprised *me* was your insistence that I pay a bond *plus* an extra five dollars a week!'

'Well, I figured with the rent you were getting for your apartment you could easily afford it!'

Kelly dug her fingernails into the palms of her hands as she again struggled to contain herself. 'Why don't you sit down?' she invited between clenched teeth and indicated the chair covered with the two white towels. 'I'll get us some lemonade.'

'Thanks, that would be very nice,' he said, masking his surprise at her sudden hospitality. He sat down on the edge of the battered old monstrosity, leaning slightly forward, forearms resting comfortably on his well-muscled thighs, huge hands clasped loosely between his knees as he watched Kelly perform her simple tasks.

Her hair swung against her cheek when she reached into the Esky for the bottle of lemonade. She quickly raised a slender hand and impatiently tucked it behind one shell-like ear. Her movements were light and graceful as she filled two tall glasses with the beverage, and when she returned the bottle to the Esky, her hair once more fell against her cheek. Jack wondered if she would tuck it back again, and when she did, the corners of his mouth lifted in a grin.

Kelly looked up, caught him watching her, and her heart did an unexpected leap in her chest. She quickly picked up the two glasses, handed him one, pulled out a chair from the table, straddled it and sat facing him.

Jack raised his glass. 'Cheers!' He emptied the vessel, placed it on the floor and eased his huge frame farther back into the chair.

'Comfy?' Kelly murmured, knowing by his sudden expression of dismay that he had finally encountered that totally wicked spring! She smiled, raised her glass and sipped daintily at her lemonade.

'*Good grief*! Where did you get this blasted thing?' Jack demanded as he shifted uncomfortably in the chair, searching in vain for a safer position.

'It was here when I moved in.' She took another dainty sip of lemonade. 'I guess that means it's yours.'

He glowered at her. 'Have you ever sat in this thing?'

'Just the once,' she replied in round-eyed innocence.

'Well, it's downright dangerous! You should throw it out!'

'Throw it out!' She looked shocked. 'But it's my only chair. Where would my guests sit? Besides, if I threw it out, you would most likely deduct it from my bond.'

'Enough!' he exploded and shot from the chair, two giant steps effectively covering the distance separating them.

He gazed down at her, his look so riveting, his magnetism so compelling, his maleness so potent that it sent a wild tremor rioting throughout her body. A tell-tale warmth rushed to her cheeks and her heart somersaulted as she gazed helplessly into his eyes.

'You're such a little vixen!' he growled and removed the glass from her hands and placed it on the table, his eyes holding her own. His huge hand encircled her face, tilted it upwards, and she felt herself drowning in his eyes and knew he would kiss her and knew she would be powerless to stop him.

Her lips parted voluntarily and she felt, actually felt herself floating upwards, to press her body against his, to meet the darkly sensual mouth that would claim her own. Her whole being was consumed with a wild inner excitement she had never before experienced. His hand moved from her face to the slender column of her throat, his hard fingers caressing the delicate skin at her nape before tangling themselves in the silky abundance of her hair. She arched her head back, her lids closing over her eyes, her lips trembling with a throbbing eagerness as she waited breathlessly for the touch of his mouth against hers.

'You're so beautiful, Kelly,' he murmured huskily, his breath hot against her cheek. 'So fiery...so bewitching.'

Her arms went up to encircle his neck, her fingers splaying through the coarse texture of his hair, and when his mouth closed finally over hers she returned the kiss with a passion every bit as fierce as his own. His hands slipped under her sweater to explore the delicate skin of her back and sides before coming to rest with a tantalising closeness beneath the swell of her breasts, and her breath caught in her throat before she gasped in delight.

He picked her up and carried her into the bedroom. Kelly clung to him, her arms wrapped tightly around his neck, her mouth locked to his. He lowered her gently onto the mattress, removed her sweater, and his hands slid smoothly down the silky texture of her quivering stomach to unfasten first the button and then the zipper of her jeans.

And it was the sound of the zipper being ripped urgently apart combined with the feel of the rough fabric being eased over her hips that finally jolted Kelly to her senses. Her eyes flew open and she stared in disbelieving horror into the handsome face of the man she loathed. For several seconds she could only lie there, stunned, shocked, as his long, tapered fingers moved under the lacy band of her panties, his hands appearing almost black against the pale marble smoothness of her tummy.

'What do you think you're *doing*?' she shrieked accusingly, and shoved him away with a strength she didn't know she possessed. She grabbed her sweater, pulled it over her head and raced into the lounge room. She quickly buttoned and zipped her jeans and whirled to face him as he leaned against the doorway of the bedroom, an angry flush raging across his hard cheeks, his eyes glittering like frosty blue chips in the dark storm of his face.

How could she have allowed the situation to get so out of hand? she wondered desperately. He had *touched* her, *stroked* her, *kissed* her! He had filled her with a wild, all-consuming passion beyond her wildest dreams.

And that was the problem. She'd had her fair share of involvements, none of them truly satisfying, lukewarm romances that hadn't gone anywhere, that had left her with a feeling of relief when they were ended. Until now she had foolishly believed great lovemaking could only occur with someone you truly loved, worshipped, adored. Jack Saunders had robbed her again! He had stolen her ideal, her precious belief. She didn't love him. She detested him! She pressed her trembling hands to her throbbing temples.

'Get out!' she whispered hoarsely.

'Not a chance!' He pushed himself away from the door and walked slowly towards her.

Kelly backed away. 'Please!' she begged. 'Please don't...'

'Make love to you?' He shook his dark, unruly head and added coldly with a contemptuous smile, 'The mood, the moment, the magic...has somehow disappeared!'

He stood in front of her, so totally male, so potently virile, so strong and handsome. Had she done that to his hair, mussed it like that? Her nostrils twitched, assailed with his intoxicating male scent, so clean, so fresh, so... She took another hasty step backwards. *Magic*? More like *witchcraft*!

'I . . . I'm sorry,' she said helplessly, looking miserably away from him. 'I didn't mean for this to . . . to happen.'

His eyes blazed. 'No?'

'No!' she whispered.

'Then what *did* you mean to happen?' he demanded harshly.

'N-Nothing.'

'Nothing?' His short, sharp bark of disbelieving laughter filled the small room. 'Come on, Kelly, you can do better than that! You were *waiting* for me. You obviously wanted *something*!'

So he had seen her on the veranda and had deliberately chosen to ignore her, forcing her to go to him. 'Surely you don't think I . . . I *planned* for you to . . . to attack me?'

'Attack you?' he snorted. 'Hardly! A man rarely finds such an eager partner!'

Her eyes blazed. 'You're disgusting!'

His hand shot out and grabbed her wrist. 'No more love talk! Let's get down to some *serious* discussion. What happened to your business?'

As if he didn't already know! 'Your sparkling performance on television killed it!'

'Don't give me all the credit! I warned you about that tongue of yours getting you into trouble.'

'*My tongue!*' she flared. 'Good grief, you're totally insufferable. It was your tongue that did it . . . not mine. You deliberately manoeuvred that interview so I *couldn't* speak, couldn't properly explain myself!'

'You had already said too much,' he growled, and when she opened her mouth to issue the hot retort sizzling on her lips, he raised a hand and incredibly it was enough to silence her. 'So your business has hit a low.

I thought as much.' He raised a hand and dragged it roughly through his hair. 'It will bounce back. People have short memories. Eventually you will be forgiven,' he added arrogantly and raised his hand again to warn her into a shuddering silence. 'The question is, where do you go from here?'

Kelly took a deep breath, swallowed her pride and prayed he wouldn't make her beg.

'If... if you would give me a job then people would think everything is all right between us, that... that it was only a misunderstanding.' She added fervently, 'And it was! I thought you would use subcontractors, otherwise I would never have put in a bid.'

His deep blue eyes narrowed shrewdly on her face as he considered her words. 'What sort of job did you have in mind?'

Hope sprang to her eyes and her heart skipped several beats. He was actually asking if she had a *preference*!

'Well, I have a degree in science with a double major in biology and botany. I'm only telling you this so you will know I'm fully qualified and... and you did say I had plenty of imagination and flare,' she quickly reminded him.

'I remember!' he growled impatiently. 'And now perhaps you might remember to answer my question by kindly telling me what sort of job you have in mind?'

A deep flush stained Kelly's cheeks and she almost choked on the pride she had swallowed earlier. 'I... I noticed when you were inspecting your gardens that you seemed rather displeased with several of the plants and shrubs.' She cleared her throat, wanting to sound firm and business-like, not begging or pleading. 'You could hire me to replace any plants you don't like with ones you do and . . . and generally look after things,' she finished in a rush.

There, she had done it. She had asked for his help. She held her breath, anxiously searching his eyes for a positive reaction.

'You were obviously mistaken. I like *all* my plants.'

'No, you don't!'

'I most certainly do!'

'You do *not*! I saw how you looked when you were writing in your notepad,' she stated accusingly. 'You were obviously angry, upset . . . annoyed.'

He chuckled and withdrew the pad from his back pocket. 'You misread me. Unlike you, I'm not a botanist.' He took her fingers in his huge hand and placed the pad, opened, in her palm. 'I sometimes have difficulty remembering the botanic names for some of the plants I especially like and want included in other projects . . . so I simply take their names from the tags in order not to forget them.'

Kelly stared bleakly down at the bold black scrawls on the small white pages. *Bauhinia blakeana* . . . *Metrosideros* . . . *Dampiera* . . . and realised with a jolt that several of his favourite plants were also her own.

'But I could still take care of the upkeep,' she pleaded, no longer caring if she sounded desperate. 'The weeding . . . the watering . . .'

'The contractors who designed the project are also responsible for the upkeep.'

'I see,' she whispered and swallowed hard. 'So . . . so there's no job?'

'Afraid not.'

Kelly handed him back the notepad and turned quickly away from him but he had already witnessed the tears sparkling on her lashes. He frowned darkly and shoved the pad roughly into his pocket. The frown deepened. Perhaps he *had* been too hard on her at the interview. An unexpected wave of remorse swept over him.

'I'm building an island resort in the Whitsundays,' he stated gruffly. 'There's a job there if you want it.'

Kelly turned slowly, hardly daring to believe her ears. 'There is? You really mean it?' She could see he did. She wanted to hug him. Instead, she impulsively grabbed his two huge hands in the small enclosures of her own and held tightly on to them. 'Thank you, Jack! Thank you so *much*.' She knew she was blubbering but simply couldn't help herself. 'I'll be one of the best darned gardeners you've ever hired!'

'Hold on! I said there was a job! I didn't say anything about gardening. Construction has barely begun. It will be several months before any landscaping is possible, and when it is, I'll be using the same firm as here.'

Confusion clouded her eyes. 'But... but you said...'

'I said there was a *job*!'

'What... what sort of job?'

'How good are you at cooking?'

'*Cooking*?'

He nodded. 'I suppose, like most women, you're pretty good at it, huh?'

Kelly stared up at him, hardly believing he could make such a chauvinistic remark. 'I suppose,' she muttered and dropped his hands in disgust.

'Right now,' he continued, blissfully unaware that anything was amiss, 'there are only a couple of men operating heavy machinery, preparing the site, but next week I'll be sending in my construction crews. I'll need someone to take charge of supplies, cook, serve and clean up.'

A *slave*! He wanted a slave for himself and his crew. She pictured herself stirring an enormous stew in a huge black cauldron sweltering over an open fire somewhere in a cluster of tropical islands, most of them deserted, surrounded only by the sea. She pictured herself peeling mountains of potatoes, washing endless stacks of dishes, scrubbing soot-blackened pots and being half eaten alive by sandflies and mosquitoes. This man must hate her as much as she hated him!

Still, it was a job! Not the sort of job she had been hoping for... but a job nonetheless.

'What... what about the pay?'

He told her and she gasped aloud. With that kind of money she could easily pay off all her bills, make double payments on her mortgage each month and build up her bank account! Of course it would mean slaving for the devil himself at something she had never done before, had never even considered doing but... *it was a job* and she was grateful. The trick now was not to appear overly eager.

'I accept!' she blurted. 'When do I start?'

'In a week. I'll pick you up here. Our only access to the island is by barge or plane. We'll go by plane,' he added as an afterthought. 'Once you've completed the cooking contract, I'll have a look at some of your gardening ideas. I might be able to use you on some of my smaller projects.'

Her heart caught in her throat and her eyes glowed. This was getting better and better! A job now with a salary she had never dreamed possible and a promise of future jobs later. *Please, God*, she silently prayed, *don't let this turn out to be only a dream*!

'Thank you,' she murmured humbly, and clasped her hands in front of her in a gesture of sheer gratitude. 'I would certainly appreciate if you did that.'

He grinned, doing strange things to her heart. 'So I have a cook?'

'You have a cook.'

His blue-black eyes held hers for several long, nerve-tingling seconds before he took out his notepad again, jotted down a telephone number and handed her a slip of paper.

'You can reach me on that number. Think carefully about what you're getting yourself into, Kelly.' He added crisply, 'You've got a week to change your mind.' He crossed over to the door, opened it, and his eyes seemed to challenge her from across the room. 'Once you're on the island,' he added warningly, 'there's no turning back!'

CHAPTER THREE

THE *Jabiru*, a small, two-seater, ultra-light sport aircraft, named after Australia's only stork, flew with an easy grace beneath the fluffy white clouds and above the scenery below, which was absolutely breathtaking.

Rich green canefields gave way to glorious golden beaches, the sands playing host to the rolling surf splashing across its shores. The ocean was a sparkling blue, capped with crisp white foam, and the farther north they flew along the Great Barrier Reef towards the Whitsundays, the deeper the colour grew until finally the water took on a vibrant turquoise hue and the sands lost their golden sheen and became a breathtaking sugar white.

But the magical scenery below wasn't sufficient to allow Kelly to forget for an instant that the handsome devil at her side, dressed casually in pale beige slacks and a burgundy-coloured silk short-sleeved shirt, was actually Jack Saunders piloting the plane. Up here, floating so peacefully through the bright blue sky, with the wispy little clouds dancing shyly by their windows, it seemed as if they were all alone in a strangely beautiful, mystically exotic, universe. The notion was both thrilling and terrifying.

Sometimes his huge broad shoulders would accidentally brush against hers while he handled the controls and Kelly would immediately stiffen and wonder suspiciously if he hadn't done it deliberately. After all, she told herself, their seats weren't *that* close! But she wisely kept her suspicions to herself and her eyes trained on the beautiful scenery below.

The only time they spoke was when Jack named a passing town or community—Gladstone, Rockhampton, Mackay—nestled along the coastline or slightly inland, and she would murmur a polite acknowledgement at having heard him, nothing more. She was determined to keep their relationship on a strictly professional level. He was her boss and she was his employee. Certainly nothing complicated about that. He needed a cook and she needed a job. Simple. He had offered her that job and she had accepted it. A common, everyday business transaction. And when she had completed that job, *he would look at some of her gardening ideas*!

But when he pointed out a school of dolphins frolicking amongst the waves, Kelly forgot to maintain her polite reserve. She became so excited at seeing such a wondrous sight that Jack chuckled and obligingly brought the small aircraft down lower to give her an even better view.

He circled the group several times while the dolphins put on a dazzling display, racing backwards on their tails, leaping into the air, diving through the crisp surf and grinning cheekily up at them. When they called an end to the show and bounced away on their tails, bobbing their shining heads up and down as if taking their bows, Kelly gave them a well-deserved round of applause. She turned to Jack and, with all the exuberance of an excited child, eagerly exclaimed, 'Wasn't that just *great*?'

There was a flash of white in his deeply tanned face as he returned her smile. 'It was indeed.'

And his words were enough to make her heart continue its singing. He had enjoyed the dolphins every much as she had and for some reason these shared, uncomplicated moments had made her feel blissfully happy, fully alive and the warm glow within her continued to flow.

He looked at her beautiful, shining green eyes and realised they were almost the exact same colour as the sea below. Her glorious mane of wild auburn hair tumbled freely about her shoulders and framed the excited flush on her smooth cheeks. The pearly white of her teeth sparkled between the rosy blush of her lips. His deep blue eyes gleamed with a sudden brightness of their own and his gaze became so riveting that it was as if he was actually photographing her.

Kelly looked hastily away, then moved restlessly, knowing there was no escape from his all too disturbing presence. She had already experienced the mysterious and devastating effects this man could wield over her but she had managed, quite deliberately, during the past week, to tuck these thoughts far and firmly away, to the very back corner of her mind, where they had lain almost forgotten as she had busied herself with the task of preparing for her new job.

After all, there had been so much to do, so much to keep her busy. The appointment with the bank to arrange double payments on her mortgage had headed her list of priorities followed by having her gardening equipment serviced and cleaned in readiness for storage, which in itself had required several return trips to Bundaberg. She had thoroughly cleaned the beach shack, leaving it in a condition it hadn't been when she had rented it. The estate agent would have no excuse to complain about her to Jack.

These had been the big jobs but the little jobs had been every bit as time-consuming. Notifying the post office where her mail was to be directed, gaining reassurance from the letting agent that her beloved apartment would only be rented to caring and responsible people in case the present excellent tenants should happen to leave and finally sorting through her wardrobe and deciding what to pack and what to store.

She had climbed into bed at night exhausted; far too exhausted to pay any attention to the niggling voices in her head warning her that perhaps she was taking on more than she could chew; warning her that she was no match for a man like Jack Saunders!

The playful dolphins, the fantastic scenery, meant nothing now as the voices returned with a vengeance. It was only natural, she desperately tried telling herself, to be feeling apprehensive, a little bit scared when embarking upon a new job. Everybody feels this way. He's probably feeling the same way about me, wondering if he's made the right choice in hiring me, she tried convincing herself. But when she dared peep at him through the fringe of her long, silky lashes, she wasn't at all surprised to see this simply wasn't the case.

Jack Saunders was at his usual powerful best, his long, tanned fingers lightly touching the controls, his easy confidence not at all shaken, his arrogance where it usually was, in the fore! Perhaps she had imagined it! Imagined the *look* that had passed between them. The look she had actually *felt* in the lower part of her stomach. The same look she had experienced in the shack with such devastating results!

Feeling her eyes on him, Jack turned to her and smiled. 'Another few minutes and we'll be there. Straight ahead is the Whitsunday passage. We'll see it soon. The waters are calm and sheltered, perfect for sailing and cruising.'

Kelly nodded, unable to speak. He was behaving as if nothing at all had ever passed between them, neither here nor at the shack! Well, she would do the same. She straightened her shoulders and sat more upright in her seat.

'Enjoying the flight?' he added casually as though simply addressing a fellow traveller.

'Yes,' she lied, wondering when she had ever felt so oddly uncomfortable.

'I love flying,' he told her, his deep voice warm with enthusiasm. 'Especially in this little beauty! She's more economical than a car and easier to handle. I keep three on the island. They more than earn their keep.'

'That's nice.'

Jack sliced her an amused look. 'Too bad you can't fly.'

'How do you know I can't?' Her tone was suddenly defiant.

'Well, can you?'

'No.' Feeling foolish, she quickly turned her attention back to the window.

'Usually it's a requirement whenever I hire someone to work in a remote or an isolated area. It always pays to have multi-skilled staff.'

Multi-skilled staff, she thought uneasily. The only thing she was really skilled at was gardening. She certainly wasn't a skilled cook, probably not even a good cook, definitely not a great one. She had never dreamed that one day she might be cooking for a living.

The plane circled a few of the seventy-four islands that make up the Whitsundays on the spectacular Great Barrier Reef. Each island was as breathtakingly beautiful as the next, delicate emerald jewels fringed with swaying palm trees and pure white sandy beaches floating in the crystal clear waters of the Coral Sea, the sea of paradise.

Jack named some of the popular tourist resorts renowned the world over. He told her when each was built, the clientele they catered for, and some of the difficulties encountered during their construction, which he hoped to avoid. Kelly's inner turmoil slowly dissolved as she listened attentively. Everything is going to be all right, she firmly told herself but her heart gave an unexpected lurch as though it didn't believe it.

'Naturally, there won't be any mass clearing of vegetation on my island,' Jack continued, his voice charged with emotion. 'The main lodge with dining and recreational facilities will be built where the growth is the sparest and what is taken away will be replaced.'

'But what about accommodation? Surely you will need to do some wide-scale clearing for that?'

Jack shook his head. 'I'm not building motel-type or any other sort of cluster dwellings. I'm building pole houses set amongst the trees with great spaces separating them. Each pole house will have total privacy where the occupants can rest, relax, explore, swim, sunbake, do whatever takes their fancy while enjoying the illusion that the island belongs to them, that they are alone in their own island paradise!'

'Sounds wonderful,' Kelly sighed. 'I can easily imagine how business tycoons, the rich and famous with all the pressures they and their families are under would appreciate the luxury of such divine privacy and a chance to be themselves without anyone looking on. I guess the only time they would need to be with others is at mealtimes at the lodge.'

'Not even then, unless of course, that is their desire. They can dine in the main lodge, cook for themselves in their own well-stocked kitchens or, if they prefer, have someone come to their pole houses to prepare and serve their meals. The choice will be entirely theirs.'

Kelly suddenly leaned forward in her seat, her face pressed close to the tiny window. 'Which one is our...' she began eagerly. Hot colour seared her cheeks as she quickly corrected herself. '*Your* island?'

'We're approaching it now,' he said, giving no indication he had noticed the slip. 'I'll circle it if you like so you can have an overview?' His deep blue glance was enquiring.

'Oh, yes, please!' Kelly answered, her eyes shining as the most beautiful of all the islands loomed before them or so it seemed to her as Jack took the plane lower, treating her to a sight she was to remember the rest of her life!

The whole of the island rose majestically from the pristine white coral shimmering beneath the turquoise blue waters like a great precious green jewel. Tall, graceful palms, their elegant fronds swaying gently in the soft sea breezes, swept down from the sloping hills all the way to the sparkling white beaches. Towards the far end of the island was a cluster of small buildings, which, from the air, looked like a tiny village.

'Temporary dwellings,' Jack explained as they circled the complex. 'More will be added as it becomes necessary but right now we have dorm and shower facilities for approximately thirty men, mainly young apprentices and labourers. You will be responsible for feeding them. That building to the right of us is the office... or administration quarters... as Max likes to call it,' he added with a chuckle. 'Behind it is the infirmary and the relocatable homes for architects, engineers and supervisors. You won't need to worry about them, though. They're equipped to feed themselves.'

One white building, the largest by far, was well away from the rest, more nestled in the tropical glade. It looked rather interesting with its long, low flat roof and wide screened-in enclosures.

'What is that big building used for?' Kelly asked curiously.

'That's the mess. Your domain.'

Kelly's throat felt suddenly dry. 'That's the *kitchen*?' she asked in a tight-sounding voice.

'And dining room.'

Her heart thumped and her hand trembled as she raised it to her throat. The place looked big enough to cater for an army! Her mind raced. Thirty men now and possibly more to come. She wouldn't be stirring one pot, she would be stirring *hundreds*! How would she ever manage? Why hadn't she thought of this before? she thought frantically as the cold hard reality of her job finally struck her straight between the eyes.

'I'll take her down now but you can eventually explore it all at your leisure,' Jack told her as he prepared to land. 'Fasten your seat-belt,' he ordered crisply.

Kelly was all thumbs as she hastened to obey his command. But the simple procedure of inserting the clasp into the lock was now more than her suddenly clumsy fingers seemed capable of managing. With one hand and without taking his eyes from the crude runway rushing up to meet them, Jack reached over and expertly did it for her, his strong, warm fingers brushing against the trembling nervousness of her own.

The *Jabiru*'s wheels bit lightly into the hard-packed sand and rolled easily to a smooth stop. Jack patted the control panel. 'This little beauty could stop on a dime!'

Kelly's face was ashen. 'I ... I'm sure it could.'

He glanced at her sharply. 'Are you all right?' He slipped his arm firmly around her shoulders, drawing her against him, and while she knew the gesture was simply to reassure and comfort her, her heart jolted and her pulses pounded and it was all she could do to keep herself from actually snuggling into his warm embrace. His free hand lightly stroked her cheek and he gently tucked a stray lock of hair behind her ear the way she had done at the shack. Kelly squeezed her eyes shut and desperately tried to quell the dizzying currents rioting within her.

'There now, it's all over,' he soothed, comforting her as if she was a small, frightened child. 'I guess to a novice a home-made runway can seem pretty daunting,' he continued sympathetically, his warm breath fanning her cheek and kindling the fires burning within her. 'But it's a whole lot safer than it looks. You'll feel better once you get some air.'

He unfastened her seat-belt and with his hand so perilously close to the lower part of her stomach a fresh shock of awareness rippled through her. Her small, startled gasp was thankfully smothered by the sound made when he opened her door. A fresh tropical sea breeze instantly filled the small cabin and ruffled her silky hair.

'There, how's that?' he asked gruffly, his eyes resting on the glorious bounty of her hair.

'F-Fine,' she murmured, unable to hear her voice above the wild thrashings of her heart.

'Good.' He smiled and touched her hair again. It was as though he couldn't get enough of it. His blue eyes became gleaming pools of fascination as he intently watched the silky russet strands gliding smoothly between and over his fingers. Kelly stiffened and pulled away from him. His mouth hardened and he dropped his hand.

'Pull yourself together!' he ordered. 'I can't have you going all faint and woozy on me when a band of hungry men are depending on you!' He abruptly opened his door and jumped down onto the hardened sand.

Faint and woozy indeed! Indignation flared in her eyes as she watched him stride past the windscreen. *A band of hungry men depending on me*? Panic hit her again, this time worse than before. If she failed at this job there would be no chance of Jack taking a look at her gardening ideas and hiring her for some of his smaller projects. He raised his hands to help her down from the light aircraft but she couldn't move. With a muttered oath of impatience, he encircled her tiny waist, lifted her effortlessly from the plane and set her firmly down on the hard-packed sand, before retrieving her two small suitcases. Kelly's eyes darted wildly up at the *Jabiru*. She didn't want to be found out! She wanted to jump back in and take off, skill or no skill!

The wind tugged at the hem of her white skirt, lifted it and cheekily revealed a pair of long, slender legs. The same wind teased her rich, glowing auburn hair away from the fragile stem of her neck and smoothed her pink

short-sleeved blouse across her jutting breasts. Jack's
eyes darkened dangerously. She was at once both seductive and innocent.

'You will change into something far more practical
when we hit camp,' he stated in a voice that warned she
had absolutely no choice in the matter. He strode towards an opened Jeep parked in the shade of a clump
of native gum trees and tossed her suitcases into the back.
When he turned and saw she hadn't followed him, a
harsh expression leapt into his eyes and the corners of
his mouth twisted into a cynical smile. He leaned against
the Jeep and crossed his ankles.

*And she realised he knew. Knew she wasn't up to the
job. She could see it in his eyes, in his smile, in the way
he stood there, as if expecting, or daring her to run. But
there was nowhere to run.* Kelly swallowed hard and
began to walk slowly towards him, taking one small step
at a time until she was a little more than a metre away
from him. Then she stopped.

They stood silently, like sparring partners in a ring;
she against the backdrop of bright blue sky and clean
white sands, he against the rustic Jeep. The air was
charged with an explosive energy as if waiting for a
storm. Jack lifted his hand and, with his index finger,
beckoned her closer.

A deep flush rose high on Kelly's cheeks. She took an
awkward step forward and then another. Pride forced
her head up and put a smile on her face, a bright,
holiday-kind-of smile. She took a deep breath of the
clean island air and let it out slowly as if she had never
before experienced anything quite so wonderful.

'Just smell that,' she sighed in apparent ecstasy, and took another deep, satisfying breath. 'There's nothing like clean, fresh island air. I'm going to *love* it here!'

Dark brows rose mockingly above pools of glittering blue frost. 'So you're quite happy to stay?'

Her eyes widened as she appeared quite puzzled. 'Well, of course!'

'Why the sudden change of heart?'

'Change of heart?' Her eyes grew wider still. 'Whatever do you mean?'

He pushed himself away from the Jeep, crooked a finger under her chin and forced her to look at him.

'You have beautiful eyes,' he astonished her by saying. 'In fact, they're quite remarkable. I like looking at them . . . especially when they change colour. Right now, they're very green, a dark green, the same rich colour as the velvet moss that spreads across and covers the rocks in Tasmania's Central Highlands.'

Kelly stared up at him, totally thunderstruck. The last thing she'd expected was a compliment . . . and this wasn't just any old compliment. Never had her eyes been so poetically and romantically described.

'Thank you,' she murmured shyly while aware of a warm blush staining her cheeks.

'No, it is *I* who should be thanking you. I've noticed your eyes always become a deep mossy colour . . . whenever you lie!'

'Whenever I . . .' The flush of her pleasure drained swiftly from her face and she became noticeably pale.

'You're not going to love it here, you're going to hate it!' he stated with an icy calmness.

The words were so softly spoken that at first Kelly didn't grasp their terrifying significance, but when she did, panic rose again in her throat. 'Is...is that your intention?' she demanded shakily. 'That I should h-hate it?'

'My intention was to hire a cook!' he exploded angrily, fury dancing in his eyes. 'You were given a week to think it over. Your silence was your acceptance.' His eyes burned into her own and his hand moved down to snare her wrist. 'I warned there was no turning back,' he issued tightly. 'Didn't I make myself clear?'

The panic rioting within her formed a frenzied knot in her stomach. 'Y-Yes, yes, you did. A-Absolutely!' she stammered.

He gazed into her eyes for several more seconds before he abruptly released her. 'Good. Now get into the Jeep.'

But Kelly could only stand there, staring up at him, her beautiful green eyes filled with the realisation that he was right. There *was* no turning back. She was *trapped*!

'Now!' he exploded.

Without taking her eyes from his cold, angry face, Kelly quickly climbed into the Jeep. Jack slid in beside her and turned the key already in the ignition. 'Fasten your seat-belt,' he ordered curtly.

When she reached up and tugged at the shiny metallic clasp next to her head, the darn thing refused to budge. 'It...it's stuck.'

With a sigh of impatience, Jack effortlessly freed the clasp and brought the belt down and around her in one swift and easy movement. The Jeep ploughed through the narrow track, slipping and sliding through the starchy white sand forming great drifts as they went. It would have been fun had the atmosphere not been so tense. Kelly held on to the edge of her seat, eyes glued straight ahead, grateful for the snug fit of the seat-belt that kept her from falling against him. Another long, sweeping curve and suddenly the Jeep was on hardened ground, the soft sand graded and packed down.

This smoother track led them into the cluster of buildings seen from the air. Jack brought the Jeep to a shuddering halt directly in front of one of them. Another Jeep, identical to the one they were in, was parked alongside the veranda rail. Jack sprang from the vehicle and opened the door.

'Get out!' he ordered sharply.

With her head held high, and without even noticing the curious glances they were receiving from the various groups of men supposedly going about their own business, Kelly stepped gracefully down and disdainfully ignored the strong, tanned hand that had reached out to assist her. Jack muttered under his breath, grabbed her cases from the back of the Jeep and dropped them with a loud clatter onto the wooden floor of the veranda.

'This is the administration building.' His sharp, accusing eyes ripped over her and it became more than Kelly could bear. Her gaze faltered and her lower lip trembled and she was finally forced to look away.

'Max will settle you in,' he added with a sinister softness and she shivered because it sounded like the devil himself had parted her hair and whispered the ominous words straight into her ear.

Kelly stumbled blindly up the three steps leading onto the veranda. She walked stiffly past her two suitcases and pushed open the screened door. The Jeep tore away behind her, leaving in its wake a swirling cloud of white dust.

She could only pray that Max was a decent sort of fellow. The sort of fellow who would see at a glance that she was not cut out to be a chef. The sort of man who would heartily recommend that she be given some other job.

A tiny spark of hope ignited in Kelly's chest. That way she would save face...and still be in for a chance at having Jack look at her gardening ideas.

CHAPTER FOUR

THE administration quarters was merely a fancy term for a sparsely furnished reception area with a small office space behind a counter and another office at the back. The floor consisted of rough wooden planks and the walls and ceiling were simply sheets of fibreglass joined together at their seams.

Two uncomfortable-looking black chairs pushed sharply against a wall were enough to warn any unsuspecting visitor that prolonged stays weren't welcomed. There were no windows, the only natural light coming from the front and back opened screened doors. A huge fan hung from the ceiling, its blades mindlessly rotating the hot, still air.

The counter, broken only by a small walk through, divided the reception area from the working area. Seated at a huge cluttered desk behind the counter was a solidly built, middle-aged woman, with short, straight, greying brown hair, parted to one side and held in place with a large, black leather clip. She was dressed in a pair of faded blue jeans and a short-sleeved red plaid cotton shirt. Work boots, similar to the ones Kelly wore on gardening jobs, adorned her feet, while a pair of rimless spectacles squatted dangerously close to the tip of her long nose.

A fax machine chugged out a message close to her elbow. The woman glanced at it sharply, reading it swiftly while still speaking rapidly into the mouthpiece of a telephone held snugly against her chest with her chin. Her hands were busy on the keyboard of a computer, her blunt fingers a blur of motion dancing across the keys. Kelly watched, totally fascinated, not daring to disturb her. This unlikely-looking secretary was one heck of a worker!

'Well, missy, don't just stand there gawking. State your business.'

It took Kelly a few seconds to realise the words were addressed to herself, that the woman had concluded her telephone conversation and was now peering at her over the rims of her glasses with sharp, bright, berry brown eyes. Kelly stepped quickly up to the counter, a flush of embarrassment staining her cheeks for she knew she had indeed been guilty of gawking.

'Mr... Mr Saunders dropped me off just now,' Kelly began hesitantly, feeling slightly intimidated and more than just a little disconcerted by the shrewd brown eyes keenly studying her, as though this woman knew just by looking at her that she wasn't much of a cook and probably incapable of providing for thirty or more hungry construction workers!

'I know. I heard the commotion.'

Kelly's flush deepened. 'Yes, well, Jack... Mr Saunders,' she quickly corrected herself when the woman's brows arched sharply, obviously disapproving of a new employee being on such familiar terms with the boss. Kelly sighed deeply and added in a small tired voice, 'I'm Kelly McGuire and Mr Saunders told me to see Max.'

'Oh, he did, did he?' The woman removed her glasses, folded them carefully and placed them on the desk.

Kelly nodded, squared her slender shoulders and returned the woman's sharp-eyed stare. 'So...where is he?'

'Who?'

'Max.'

'Sittin' right here.'

Kelly's eyes widened. 'You're...*Max*?'

'Yup.' Max chuckled, obviously enjoying Kelly's surprise. 'Maxine, really, but everyone calls me Max. I prefer it, actually. Maxine sounds a bit prissy.' Despite the amused chuckle the keen brown eyes hadn't lost their shrewdness. 'So? Why did the boss send you to me?'

Kelly hesitated. Max was obviously a champion amongst women, capable of anything and everything, the sort who believed nothing was impossible once you put your mind, or back, or cookbook, to it.

'He said you would settle me in.'

Max arched her brows in surprise, picked up her glasses and polished them on the hem of her plaid shirt. 'Well, that's a departure, I must say. He always settles his ladies in himself.'

'If it's too much trouble I could settle myself in. You need only point me in the right direction and...'

Max stood up and treated herself to a leisurely stretch. There was not an ounce of excess flesh on her huge frame. She was really quite majestic, Kelly decided admiringly. 'It's too far to walk, especially in this heat, and I could do with a break. Besides, it never pays to go against the boss's wishes.'

Kelly nodded and sighed. 'Don't I know it!'

'Displeased him already, huh?' Max chuckled softly. 'I thought as much...judging from the clatter out there!' She grabbed a wide-brimmed stockman's hat from a peg on a wall near the overcrowded desk, plonked it squarely on her head and joined Kelly on the other side of the counter. 'Have you much luggage?'

'Two small suitcases. They're outside on the veranda.'

Max picked up both bags despite Kelly's protests that she could manage. The bags were tossed into the back of the parked Jeep and Kelly climbed into the passenger seat next to Max. The keys were already in the ignition just like they had been at the airstrip. Obviously, no one worried about thefts on an island, Kelly decided and smothered a sigh. After all, how would they escape? Where would they hide?

The Jeep swooped past the dormitory and the small single dwellings. Several people waved, but instead of waving back, Max preferred to toot the horn. While she was a capable driver, she was also an enthusiastic one and Kelly was grateful on more than one occasion for the seat-belt that kept her from being tossed overboard. Within minutes they had left the temporary dwellings behind and were bumping along on a narrow, sandy track leading into the thick green tropical shrubbery.

Conversation was rendered impossible due to the roughness of the ride and so Kelly didn't question Max as to where she was taking her although she couldn't help but be surprised that they had left civilization, such as it was, behind. She could only be grateful that Max hadn't taken her up on her offer to get to her accommodation by herself. The tropical heat and the weight of her suitcases would have made even a relatively short journey rather difficult.

The Jeep roared into a small but shaded clearing, and nestled within a clump of palm trees on the edge of a beautiful inlet was a rather splendid-looking caravan or mobile home. A veranda jutted out from the front of it, looking onto the small secluded beach, the pure white sand stretching out to meet the fantastic shimmering turquoise hues of the water.

The Jeep came to a halt beside the caravan and Kelly jumped out immediately, her eyes sparkling with excitement. With accommodation like this and her own private beach she would quite happily and even cheerfully put up with anything Jack Saunders tossed her way. She would stir a hundred pots, *thousands*!

Max retrieved Kelly's suitcases and headed for the caravan, again refusing Kelly's offer to help. 'The door will be open,' she said in her attractive Queensland drawl and carried the cases into the van while Kelly stood on the veranda and looked again at her view.

The palm trees rustled gently in the soft tropical sea breezes while the waters lapped the quiet, peaceful shore of the crystal white sand. Overhead, the sky was a cloudless blue. Glorious! Wonderful! Fantastic! When she entered the caravan, her delight was compounded.

The kitchen, dining and lounge areas boasted up-to-the-minute technology, including a small dishwasher, garbage disposal unit, television, radio and telephone. A dining table, hosting a huge cane basket filled with fresh tropical fruits, separated the kitchen from the lounge area with its sumptuous-looking, deep-cushioned chocolate brown leather lounge suite, coffee tables and lamps. The bedroom was equipped with a king-size bed, spacious closets and private bathroom. Everything, every commodity, every convenience one could expect to find in a luxury unit was incorporated into the caravan and Kelly couldn't help being dazzled by it all.

'It's all so very grand!' she exclaimed as she sat down on the edge of the king-size bed and ran her hands gently over the luxurious and obviously very expensive royal blue satin spread. 'I wasn't expecting anything like this. To tell you the truth, Max, I was quite prepared for nothing more than a cot in a tin shed!'

Max surprised her by throwing back her head and roaring with laughter. 'You're quite a treat, Kelly McGuire. Now, why don't you unpack and have a wee rest? You look mighty tired to me.'

'A rest?' It was just what she needed. She had risen at five that morning and the strain of the past few hours plus the uncertainty of the past couple of months had more than taken their toll. She felt she could sleep for a week but now was not the time. She got up, glanced longingly down at the comfortable-looking bed and shook her head. 'No, I must think about lunch.'

Max chuckled. 'There's plenty of food in the refrigerator if you're hungry. I stocked it myself only an hour ago.'

'Not for me, Max. For the others.'

Max frowned. 'What others?'

'Why the construction crew, of course.'

'The construction crew?' Again Max chuckled. 'Don't you go worryin' your pretty little head about them. Have yourself a wee kip and I'll see you later.'

After Max roared off in the Jeep, Kelly stood on the veranda savouring the sweet-scented, spicy island air. The coconut palms rustled in the warm tropical sea breezes while a flock of rainbow lorikeets, with their brilliant lime green bodies, scarlet breasts, yellow neckbands and royal blue heads, screeched amongst the fronds. A delighted grin spread across her face and for a moment she forgot her tiredness and her worries and, above all, the inner tensions she had been feeling ever since she had first laid eyes on Jack Saunders. Tensions that had heightened dramatically and dangerously now that she was actually under his control, an extremely well-paid employee!

The luxury of the caravan had taken her by surprise. She had meant every word when she told Max she hadn't expected anything so grand. The caravan, this beautiful setting, well, it made her feel special, as if Jack had gone out of his way to make up for what he had done to her. He could just as easily have put her in one of the dormitories, perhaps even had her share with Max, but, no, he had provided her with her own luxurious accommodation, her own mobile home, where she could enjoy peace and quiet at the end of her long, hard days. She felt grateful to him, not only for this wonderful place but also for the job and the chance afterwards and now she wished with all her heart that she could tell him so.

Tell him thank you. Tell him she would work hard, do her very best. Tell him she was sorry she had behaved the way she had earlier and that his people would never know she wasn't a highly trained chef. She vowed, then and there, that Jack Saunders would one day tell her the smartest thing he ever did...was in hiring her!

The rainbow lorikeets flew off, and with a contented sigh, Kelly turned and entered the luxurious caravan. Should she take Max's advice and have a rest, she wondered, or should she change into something more suitable and begin immediate preparations for lunch? She hesitated, undecided. Max obviously thought she should have a chance to settle in before she began the rigours of her new job.

But Max wasn't her boss, Kelly wisely reminded herself. Jack Saunders was her boss and she knew, despite her sudden warm gratitude towards the man, that this was something she mustn't forget, not even for one minute. Jack expected her to feed his crew. Starting with lunch. She wouldn't let him down. No, sirree. It didn't matter how tired or nervous or daunted she felt at the prospect of preparing her first-ever meal for anyone other than herself or for a few close friends who really didn't care what you put in front of them as long as the conversation was great! It didn't matter. What mattered was pleasing the boss!

Kelly glanced at the small leather-strapped wristwatch circling her slender wrist. It was early yet. Really much too early to begin lunch. Lunch was probably only a salad anyway and something as easy as that would take no time at all to prepare.

She had time to unpack, have a shower, and then maybe, just maybe, lie down for a few minutes so she would at least appear rested, and then change into something...*chefy*...and follow the track back to the mess. There would still be plenty of time left to become acquainted with the kitchen before getting out the lettuce and tomatoes, bread and butter, probably some cold meat. With that decision made, Kelly unbuttoned her blouse in preparation for her shower as she walked into the bedroom. Her eyes fell immediately upon the enormous king-size bed.

She had sat on it and it had certainly *felt* comfortable but was it really? She pressed down on it with her hand. Yes, the mattress was definitely firm. She loved a firm mattress. Nothing eased the muscles more after a grueling day's work than the support of a good hard mattress. Still, to be sure, one had to actually lie on a bed to judge its worth. Kelly kicked off her shoes and stretched out, then turned on her back and gave it the ultimate test. *Bliss*! She could actually feel the stiffness seeping out of her muscles, the tensions within her slowly dissolving. The coconut palms rustled softly in the sea breezes and the waves lapped gently across the shores. *Ecstasy*! Her eyelids grew heavy and started to close.

Just a few minutes, she thought drowsily. Just a few minutes...then I'll unpack...have my shower...lay out something practical that Jack...bless him...will be sure to approve of...and...and *then* I'll lie down, just to relax a little, not...not to sleep...lunch... tomatoes...lettuce...Jack...glad he hired me...all that money...and his promise...Jack...

Kelly frowned in her sleep. Such a dreadful noise. It sounded rather like a Jeep or a trail bike...which was very strange...because neither of these had a place in her dream. The noise continued to disturb her and she turned her head restlessly from side to side in order to escape it. Her hair fanned out about her face and spread across the blue satin spread like silky wings of fire. The distracting noise mercifully stopped and Kelly sank gratefully into her dream, a soft smile immediately replacing her frown.

She was in a huge auditorium, wearing an elegant white evening gown, standing in the centre of a stage, practically blinded by the television cameras and the spotlights blazing down on her. In her arms was an enormous bouquet of red and white roses. She was smiling and waving at the crowd, blowing them kisses. They were giving her a standing ovation, cheering wildly, shouting out her name...for she had just been awarded Jack Saunders's prestigious and highly coveted Chef of the Universe Award!

Jack was standing beside her, breathtakingly handsome in his tuxedo, the bright lights casting glimmering shades of blue across his raven black hair. He was clapping and cheering as wildly as everyone else, his deeply tanned face split into a dazzling white smile, and when her eyes shyly, modestly, met his, she could see the pride in them and her pounding heart swelled with joy until she thought it would surely burst. He continued to shout out her name, his voice ringing louder and truer than all the others. *Kell-ee! Kell-ee! Kell-ee!*

'*KELLY!*'

Kelly's long, silky lashes fluttered as gently as the wings of a butterfly against the smoothness of her cheeks before her eyes slowly blinked open. Jack was standing over her, his huge, warm hands gripping her shoulders. Her eyes became iridescent pools of green as she smiled sleepily, happily, up at him. 'Hi,' she whispered dreamily and reached up to stroke his hard cheek, her fingers moving lightly down the strong, tanned column of his neck to touch the collar of his burgundy silk shirt. 'You've changed out of your tuxedo!' she pouted.

Jack grabbed her hand and his sudden abrupt movement startled her and she became fully awake. Only then did she dimly realise that the darkly handsome face glaring down at her bore no resemblance, no resemblance whatsoever, to the handsome face that had beamed proudly down at her only moments before. Her eyes clouded with confusion and then cleared. She had been dreaming! The prestigious award, the beautiful gown, the magnificent roses, the accolades, Jack's pride in her, the way he had looked at her, *especially* the way he had looked at her, had all been a dream, nothing but a dream, a silly dream. The black fury sparkling like demons in his eyes told her that the fairy-tale dream had truly ended ... that this ... this was reality!

'What in blazes do you think you're doing?' he exploded. 'I turn my back on you for half an hour and you sneak around here and go to *sleep*!' He shook his head as though he couldn't quite believe it and pulled her to her feet. 'I thought you meant it when you said you wanted a job.'

'I did mean it!'

His eyes bristled with contempt as he continued to glare down at her. 'Well, if this is any indication of how hard you intend to work then I should sack you!'

'Well, why don't you?' Kelly shot back, her own eyes blazing with defiance. 'I don't want to work for you. I never did. I only asked for a job in the first place because I was desperate ... and I only agreed to *this* job because of the *money*!'

A deathly silence filled the still air. Kelly could actually hear her own heart pounding in her ears. Jack pulled her roughly against his chest, his fingers like hard bands of steel gripping her shoulders, his eyes like shards of ice piercing her face.

'Nothing,' he rasped, 'nothing would give me greater pleasure than to put you on the next plane or barge out of here and be done with you. Unfortunately, that would be too easy. Therefore, I must deny myself that pleasure.'

He released her so abruptly that Kelly staggered backwards and fell onto the bed. Her hair swirled in a shimmering, fiery halo about her face and shoulders. She pushed it back with trembling hands and continued to glare boldly up at him.

'Why must you deny yourself that pleasure?' she taunted. 'I can't imagine you denying yourself *anything*!'

A lesser woman would surely have cowered under the potency of his fury but not Kelly. She watched, fascinated, as his hands clenched and unclenched at his sides, stared as though still in her dream at the small muscles twitching spasmodically alongside the hard line of his jaw and she knew with a sudden wild panic what it was costing him to maintain his rigid control and what might happen if he released it!

His blue-black eyes sliced to the front of her opened blouse. 'I suppose you're right,' he agreed softly, his voice laced with a silky-smooth sarcasm. 'I really can't deny myself anything...especially when it's offered so freely, so enticingly.' With both hands, he reached down and traced the white lacy edge of her bra.

The movement was so outrageously deliberate and so unexpected that Kelly could only sit there, stunned, shocked, electrified, her breath leaving her lungs in a startled gasp while a thrill of anticipation danced crazily along her spine.

Her eyes, smoky with the passion he had so effortlessly aroused in her, rose helplessly to meet his and it was the cold mockery she witnessed in his own that mercifully saved her.

Kelly jumped up from the bed, tears of humiliation blinding her as she pushed him out of her way and ran to the other side, her back facing him as she struggled to fasten the buttons of her blouse. She couldn't believe it when she heard the unmistakable sounds of a huge body stretching itself out on the bed.

Her bed!

Such *nerve*!

She spun and faced him, hurt and humiliation taking a back seat now as she angrily watched him grab her pillows and bunch them behind his head. She listened in disgust to the sighs of pleasure drifting across his lips and then glared in outrageous indignation as he contentedly folded his huge tanned hands across his broad chest and...closed his eyes! Fury spread like red-hot lava throughout her entire being.

'I want you to *leave*!' She threw the words at him as if they were poisoned darts. 'Do you *hear* me?'

'I hear you,' he drawled without opening his eyes.

She glared helplessly down at him. 'I meant...*now*!'

'I'm sure you did.' He made no attempt to stifle a yawn.

'You're wrinkling the spread!' she hotly accused.

'It's wrinkleproof.'

'It doesn't matter. I don't want you on it.'

'Tough!'

Her urgent desire to smother him overcame her. She snatched a pillow from under his head. His hand shot out and grabbed a fistful of fiery auburn hair, pulling her down close to his face. They stared into each other's eyes. Then he flipped her onto her back and leaned over her, his hands imprisoning hers on either side of her head.

'I should take you now!' he rasped. 'Make love to you and then toss you out!' Anger, laced with desire, rocked in his eyes, making them appear almost satanic. 'You're a cheap little flirt, the worst kind, a tease, a troublemaker, an opportunist, a money-grubber!' His eyes gleamed down at her. 'What a tempting little morsel you made,' he continued softly, 'lying here on my bed, halfundressed, waiting for me.'

He abruptly released her and drew back in disgust. 'We'll make a deal. When I want you, I'll let you know.

You will come here . . . and afterwards, depending upon your performance, I'll pay you what I thought you were worth!' His smile became harder and crueler still. 'Naturally, the better the performance, the better the pay. We'll call it . . . *overtime*!'

He traced the line of her burning cheek and ran his fingers lightly down her throat and across the curves of her breasts. 'But, remember, *only* when I call you! I'm a busy man and you're going to be an extremely busy woman!' He rose abruptly, pulled her up after him and added a further caution. 'Of course, it goes without saying, you're not to proposition any of my men!'

With his hand firmly on her elbow, he led her out of the bedroom, through to the adjoining lounge area and stopped abruptly when he noticed her suitcases resting on the floor next to the door.

'Don't tell me you actually thought I would allow you to move in with me?' he asked incredulously.

'N-No, no, of course n-not,' Kelly stammered. 'It . . . it was a m-mistake.'

His eyes blazed. 'Damn right it was!' He released her, picked up the cases, pushed the door open with his shoulder and held it there while Kelly walked stiffly past him. He tossed her bags into the back of the Jeep and drove her back in stormy silence to the administration quarters.

This time he took no chances. With both suitcases tucked under one arm, and with his hand gripped firmly around her wrist, Jack escorted Kelly up the stairs, whisked her across the veranda and ushered her into the office, kicking the door shut behind them before dropping her suitcases to the floor. Max stood behind the counter, eyes rounded in astonishment.

'I don't know *what* she said to you, Max, and I don't want to know. Assign her a room in the dorm then get her started in the kitchen.' He peered down his long, arrogant nose at Kelly and added angrily, 'She's already wasted enough of everyone's time.'

'The kitchen!' Max repeated, bewildered. Her eyes darted from Kelly's deathly white face to Jack's glowering black one. 'But I *thought* . . . I *assumed*.' Her hands rose high then dropped in a gesture of sheer and utter helplessness. '*Hell*!'

'That's all right, Max,' Kelly said gently. 'You thought I was his girlfriend!' She picked up her two suitcases and, with head held high, started for the door. 'I can find my own way to the dorm. Lunch will be served shortly!'

CHAPTER FIVE

THE hot noonday sun blazed down on Kelly's unprotected head, adding to her discomfort. She stood stiffly in the centre of the square, a small, slender statue, gripping her suitcases. Open, flat tray trucks roared into the camp, dropped off workers and roared out again, presumably to pick up more. Some simply looked at Kelly with an open curiosity while others grinned, winked, and nudged their companions.

Kelly knew why. They apparently thought like Max, that she was the boss's woman, his latest camp companion. And she couldn't help but wonder how many women over the years had been flow in and out of various sites to be pleasured by him. Well, they would learn soon enough that Kelly McGuire was here to cook for her living and certainly not as a...*convenience* for their boss.

But it wasn't only the heat, the inquisitive glances and the soft, powdery sand shifting in and out of her white open-toed sandals that totally caused Kelly's discomfort. The administration quarters were behind her and behind that was the dormitory.

She should have taken the back door instead of the front when she made her heroic departure! Now she needed to turn around and retrace her steps. She wondered if Jack was watching her and felt certain she could feel his wicked blue eyes boring into her back. Well, she couldn't stand here much longer feeling foolish. There was a job to do.

Kelly turned quickly on her heel and, with head held high, marched back towards the administration quarters and, without even so much as a glance at the building, circled it and continued her march across the powdery white sand and up the front steps of the long veranda with its row of brightly painted green doors leading into the various rooms of the dormitory.

But which door, which room, was hers? *Damn*! She should have waited for Max. Perspiration trickled freely down her spine. She dropped her suitcases and ran the palm of her hand across her brow. Her face was a bright pink from heat and exertion and tiny ringlets of hair clung damply to her cheeks. She would kill for a cold shower. From across the compound a bell rang. Panic rose within her. Good grief! Was that the dinner bell? She reached frantically for her suitcases. Jack's shoulder brushed against hers and he strode briskly past her, swooping up her cases as he passed.

'This way,' he announced curtly and his long-legged stride halted at the far end of the shaded veranda at the very last of the bright green doors. He removed a black ring of brass keys from his hip pocket, selected one, inserted it into the lock, swung the door open, stepped inside, carrying her suitcases.

Kelly hurried after him. She stopped just inside the door, large green eyes blinking, the sudden gloomy darkness of the small room temporarily blinding her after the brilliance of the sun. The creaking sound of an alu-

minium blind rattling upwards startled her and she gave
a small gasp of alarm.

Jack stood in front of the window, the light streaming
in behind him casting deep, mysterious shadows across
the rugged planes of his face. He smiled coldly. 'Not
quite what you had in mind?'

'On the contrary,' Kelly managed with a deliberate
sweetness as she took the room in at a glance, 'this is
exactly what I had in mind!'

The small, sparsely furnished room contained a single
steel-framed bed with a blue mattress resting on top of
the wire springs. At the bottom were a set of white sheets,
pillow case and a pillow, still wrapped in plastic. Beneath the window was a small steel desk, holding a small
fan, reading lamp and a chair identical to the ones in
the reception area of the administration building. A steel
wardrobe with countless sets of initials still visible
through the fresh coat of paint that attempted to conceal
them was the only other furniture. The floor was bare
and there were no pictures on the walls.

'I love it! It's almost as good as the shack. And there's
no bond, no rent to pay!'

A dark flush spread swiftly across Jack's hard cheeks.
Kelly inwardly smiled. She knew he was punishing her
by putting her here. On a scale of one to ten, the dormitory obviously ranked the lowest. There was nothing
that could be damaged or destroyed by exuberant young
apprentices or labourers. The rooms weren't furnished
for comfort or leisure but were strictly utilitarian.

'If my memory serves me correctly,' she continued
brightly as she swooped up one of her two small cases

and hurried with it over to the bed to open and quickly retrieve her toiletry bag, 'the showers and washrooms are just around the corner. I'll have a wee wash then get straight over to the kitchen.'

Jack moved from the window and towered over her. 'A *wee wash*?' he repeated incredulously.

Kelly nodded. 'Just a quickie. I feel so hot and sticky.' She chuckled, pleased with her pun. Jack took the toiletry bag from her hand and tossed it onto the bed.

'Perhaps it might also amuse you to know that Max is in the kitchen now...doing *your* job!' he stated harshly.

'Max is doing my job?' Mental images of Max performing her own astronomical duties flashed before her. A guilty flush stained her cheeks. 'Then...then of course I must do without my wash!'

He allowed her to get almost out the door before he reached out, grabbed her hand and pulled her back. 'I can't have you making such a noble sacrifice!' He picked up the toiletry bag and placed it in her hand. 'Have your wash.'

He strode out of the room, his long strides eating up the length of the veranda. Kelly stood at the veranda rail and watched him take the steps two at a time.

'This is all your fault!' she yelled after him.

He turned slowly. 'Of course!'

'Well, it's true!' She took a deep, tremulous breath and added in a rush, 'Had you bothered to tell Max I was expected, she would never have mistaken me for one of your...your *ladies* and dragged me over to your lovenest with its king-size bed and that vulgar blue satin spread!'

'You seemed to like it!' he wickedly reminded her.

Hot colour seared her cheeks. 'Only because I thought it was mine!' She gave an indignant toss of her rich auburn mane. 'I wouldn't have gone anywhere near that van...had I known it was yours!'

'Mine *and* my ladies'!' His eyes raked boldly over her. 'Well, I needn't worry about them anymore,' he added cheerily. 'Not with you here, doing overtime!' He glanced at his watch. 'Of course, we can't start overtime until you actually begin to work!'

Kelly waited until Jack had disappeared from her view before she quickly locked the door to her room with the small key he had placed on the desk and flew across the compound towards the mess. She could hear the babble of young men's voices and see them sitting at long tables through the screened-in enclosure of the dining section. The noise ceased immediately and every head turned when she burst through the wire-meshed door.

To the right was the kitchen. Max was sitting on a stool, slouched over a counter. Kelly's eyes widened in alarm. She raced through the dining room and into the kitchen. '*Max*! Are you all right?'

Max glanced up from the magazine she was reading and peered at Kelly over the rims of her glasses. 'Sure! Why wouldn't I be?'

'I...I thought you had *fainted*! It's so hot in here.' She touched her shoulder. 'I'm sorry you had to stand in for me. I promise it won't happen again.'

Max put down her magazine and looked up at Kelly with her shrewd brown eyes. She noted how her hands were clasped too tightly in front of her; the anxious, almost desperate look in her eyes; the small beads of perspiration on her upper lip and the damp wisps of hair clinging to the hot pink of her cheeks. Max was no fool. She knew something was cooking between this lovely young woman and the Boss!

'Lunch wasn't any big deal,' Max drawled. 'Just some cold meats, salad and plenty of bread for sandwiches.' She stood up and stretched. 'They're eating fruit and ice cream for dessert.' She added with a grin, 'I used disposable plates and cups so there's no washing up. Relax, kiddo, the work's done.'

'Thanks, Max,' Kelly murmured gratefully. 'You make it all sound so simple.' She looked slowly around at the large, extremely spotless kitchen. The long, wide, stainless-steel counters shone and the huge black gas stove, with enormous pots and pans suspended on hooks above it, gleamed. There was a sudden clatter of chairs being shoved away from the tables as the men started pouring out of the dining room, taking the remainder of the fresh fruit as they went.

Kelly looked up again at the well-equipped kitchen, *her kitchen*, and nodded. 'I can do it!' she said as though speaking to herself and added firmly, convincingly, 'I *know* I can.'

'Well, any job takes some getting used to,' Max stated cheerfully as she picked up her magazine, folded it and tucked it under her arm. 'I was glad to help out today.' She started towards the door, stopped and turned around. 'Sorry about that mix-up earlier.'

Kelly lowered her eyes in embarrassment. 'It wasn't your fault, Max. You should have been told about me before I was dumped on your doorstep!'

Max chuckled. 'I *was* told about you. A week ago!'

Kelly's eyes flew to Max's face. 'A week ago?' The arrogant brute had given her a week to think it over. Obviously his chauvinism didn't include believing all women changed their minds!

'Then why... why...?'

'Why did I take you to his van?' Max chuckled as though the joke was really on herself. 'When I wrote your name down in my book, "Kelly McGuire", I pictured someone fat and jovial, a man actually, someone like we've always had on these sites. When you came in and said your name, well, I guess I wasn't really thinking or listening, just looking, and I didn't see no cook, just a pretty lady... so I settled you into the Boss's van and thought no more about it. That is—' and her brown eyes sparkled at the now-treasured memory '—until the two of you barged into my office and set me straight!'

Kelly's cheeks were scarlet. She wondered if she would ever be able to forget the whole humiliating incident. 'Yes, well, I guess it was an honest enough mistake,' she muttered and added, not wanting to let him off the hook so easily, 'but he could have at least told you I was a woman. He could have at least done *that*!'

'I guess he thought it wasn't necessary.' Max shrugged, and wondered again what was cooking between the Boss and this fiery young woman. 'He did tell me to show you where everything is stored.' She pointed briskly with the magazine at two wide and very big cupboard doors.

'That's a walk-in pantry. In it you will find such items as tea, coffee, cocoa, tinned and dry goods. Things you will use every meal.'

Kelly opened the doors for a quick peek. The shelves were loaded with sacks of sugar, flour, rice, cereals, salt, huge tins of Milo, coffee and tea, plastic containers filled with different flavoured cordials, rows of condensed milk, tomato sauces, mustards, pickles, chutneys and the like.

She followed Max into the cold room and stared in dismay at what easily seemed a hundred burlap sacks, each one almost as tall as herself, stuffed with potatoes, carrots, turnips and onions. There were blocks of cheeses, crates filled with apples, oranges, bananas, mangoes, pawpaws, pineapples, tomatoes, cucumbers, avocados, lettuces and other fresh tropical fruits and vegetables, more than her eyes could possibly take in before Max ushered her out again.

The freezer vault was next and Max explained how it was divided into sections for easy access and storage. One section was devoted entirely to king-size roasting joints: beef, pork, lamb and mutton. Another was for chops, another for steaks, another still for stewing meats, for fish and poultry, hot dogs and sausages. Huge plastic bags filled with ice cubes occupied one whole corner of the vault while shelves laden with buckets of ice cream, cakes, pies, tarts and concentrated fruit juices stretched along an entire wall.

They were both shivering when they left the freezing temperature of the vault and entered the overwhelming heat of the kitchen. 'Well, I think that takes care of most things, the important ones anyway,' Max remarked as she glanced around the kitchen. 'It won't take long before you know this place like the back of your hand.'

Her eyes stopped suddenly at a notice-board nailed to the wall beside the long, flat, barbecue section of the huge black stove. A pencil, secured with a string, dangled from the nail. Max walked over to the board and tapped it with a long finger.

'This is the meals schedule. Breakfast is at six, morning tea at nine-thirty, lunch at twelve noon, afternoon tea at three and dinner at six o'clock. The men can help themselves to supper. Just leave out some bread and jam, cakes, biscuits, whatever is left over from the day.

'Right now,' she continued, 'there are thirty in the camp but another ten will be arriving in time for dinner tonight. The numbers should stay the same for the remainder of the week but if they change, I'll let you know.' She glanced up at the wall clock hanging above the window over the sink. 'I still have a few minutes left of my lunch break. Why don't you change into something cooler? I'll stay until you get back.'

Kelly flew across the compound to the dorm, grabbed her toiletry bag, made her way to the amenities block, had a quick sponge, dashed back to her room and changed into a pair of cool cotton shorts, a loose-fitting sleeveless white blouse and blue canvas shoes. She pulled back her thick mane of hair, secured it with a wide white band, didn't bother with make-up and raced back to the dining hall.

'That certainly didn't take long.' Max chuckled approvingly but added a caution. 'Don't run around in this heat. You'll wear yourself out.'

Kelly stood at the screen door and watched Max stride briskly back across the sandy compound to the administration quarters, her heavy work boots kicking up a sandstorm as she went. A truck, loaded with two big drums, moved slowly up and down the square lightly spraying the area with water in an effort to control the never-ending swirl of fine white dust. A Jeep, driven by a deeply tanned man wearing a bright yellow construction helmet, pulled up to the administration quarters.

He had changed out of the burgundy-coloured silk shirt and beige trousers, but even so, Kelly knew immediately that the tall, superbly fit figure, dressed now in blue jeans and black T-shirt, was Jack. He jumped lithely from the vehicle and called out to Max, catching her as she was about to enter the building. They stood talking for several minutes, and even though it was impossible for Kelly to hear their conversation, she *knew* they were discussing her!

Her eyes narrowed suspiciously as she continued to watch. She felt certain Jack was questioning Max, probably to receive reassurance that Max had dutifully pointed out all the huge sacks of potatoes, carrots and onions that would eventually be scraped, peeled and chopped by her own sweet hands! Max's head bobbed up and down, obviously agreeing to everything, having nothing negative, nor even remotely disagreeable, to report about her to the Boss. Which must irk him to no

end, Kelly thought smugly and couldn't help but grin.
Good old Max!

Jack turned without warning and caught sight of Kelly
watching them from behind the screen door. The grin
froze on her face. She knew immediately he had read
her thoughts. Her first instinct was to run into the
kitchen, grab a few pots, bang them around, pretend she
was busy, working hard, sweating over the job, that she'd
been there all the time and certainly not standing idle
by the door.

But she couldn't move. He was walking straight towards her, the yellow hard-hat pushed well back from
his forehead, the bright colour in striking contrast to his
jet black hair, his dark blue eyes holding hers like two
blazing pistols! He opened the door and Kelly stepped
stiffly back, standing at rigid attention while his eyes
swept over her. Her flamboyant auburn hair tied back,
the loose-fitting white sleeveless top, the mid-thigh shorts
and even the blue canvas shoes seemed to meet with his
approval. He removed his hard hat, pulled out a chair
and tossed it onto the seat. Only then did he speak.

'I've been having a few words with Max,' he informed
her quite unnecessarily. 'She tells me you were appreciative of her standing in for you at lunch.'

Had he actually thought she mightn't have been? Two
hot spots of indignant colour rose high on her cheeks.
'Of course I was *appreciative*!' she answered tersely.

He ignored this and continued, 'She also tells me she
has shown you around the kitchen, pointed out where
most things are kept, indicated the meals schedule. Is all
this so?'

'You know it is!' Kelly answered tightly.

'Then what's the problem?' he demanded silkily.

'There aren't any problems,' Kelly returned sharply. 'But obviously you think there must be, otherwise you wouldn't be here looking like a cat about to trap a poor little mouse and it can't wait to lick its claws!'

'I've never thought of you as a poor little mouse and I doubt you would be easy to trap!' He smiled then, slow and easy, and her heart did a strange back flip in her chest. She took a hasty step backwards. The smile left his face and was replaced with a frown.

'Are you afraid of me, Kelly?' he asked softly.

The concern in his voice was so unexpected she was caught completely off guard. Afraid of him? Was she? He was big and powerful, there was no doubt about that, but it wasn't his mere physical strength that could so easily unnerve her.

It was the way he sometimes looked at her, holding her eyes for a fraction too long, so that she could still feel them on her, long after he had looked away.

It was the way he sometimes smiled at her, as he had just now, that could do such crazy things to her heart, causing it to pound and leap until she thought it must surely jump straight out of her chest.

It was the way he had kissed her at the beach shack! The remembered feel and sight of his dark hands on her body, his lips nuzzling her breasts, his hands roughly claiming her in the caravan!

It was the way he had put his arm around her in the plane when he thought she was afraid.

Afraid?

Yes, she was most definitely afraid of him. Afraid of the strange power he wielded over her... afraid because she didn't know how to protect herself against that power... afraid because she didn't know if she even wanted to!

It only took a few seconds for these thoughts to spin crazily in her head but it was long enough for her mouth to go completely dry and for her palms to grow quite damp.

'Afraid of you?' she echoed with a shaky laugh. 'What a silly question. Whatever made you *ask* such a thing? *Think* such a thing? Goodness gracious, Jack Saunders, of course I'm not *afraid* of you. Heavens, no!'

His dark brows rose above pools of twinkling blue. He chuckled softly and the warm, infectious sound washed over her and her own lips responded and curved into a hesitant smile. 'Did I protest too much?' she asked weakly.

'Perhaps. A bit. But a little fear isn't a bad thing. It can even be healthy!' He reached out and took her hands in his. She tried not to notice how little and slender and perfect they looked, tucked so snugly in the huge tanned enclosures of his own. And she valiantly ignored the tingling sensations sweeping up her forearms and bravely pretended she didn't hear the pounding of her own heart in her ears. And while she managed to do all this, she completely forgot to keep her fingers from curling tightly, possessively, around his own!

'I'm a firm but fair boss,' he told her, his voice gruff but gentle, certainly sincere. 'We got off to a rather tenuous start but we can put all that behind us now.' He smiled into her eyes and it travelled all the way to her heart, completely, totally, melting it. 'I don't want you to be afraid of me, Kelly,' he continued softly, and she shook her head to indicate she wasn't, could never be, no, not ever.

He wrapped her arms around his waist, and while she clung to him, he smoothed back tiny wisps of hair from her soft cheeks and curled fiery tendrils around his fingers before cupping her face in his hands. He bent his dark head and lightly brushed her lips with his. Her heart exploded in her chest and she strained shamelessly against him, desperately wanting more...

'I hate when I must be more firm than fair with any of my employees,' he murmured against her lips. 'But, unfortunately, sometimes that becomes necessary!' He kissed the sensitive corners of her mouth, sending delightful shivers down her spine. 'It would only occur, for example, if a particular employee felt she had an axe to grind...a score to settle!' He nibbled on her ear lobe, his sharp teeth filling her with a most exquisite pain. 'And then, of course, I would need to instil the fear of God in her!'

It took several seconds before the full extent of what he said penetrated Kelly's brain. And when it did, it was as if a bomb had been dropped on her. Her head fell back, her mouth dropped open and her eyes widened and blinked. '*What*?'

Jack reached behind him, unclasped her hands and set her firmly away from him, gripping her upper arms. 'You heard me,' he stated softly.

Kelly shook her head in bewilderment, her beautiful green eyes searching his face for some kind of understanding. Hurt and humiliation swept over her. 'You...*beast*!' she whispered hoarsely.

His hands tightened around her slender arms and his mouth hardened before he released her, picked up his hat and held it by its steel brim. His face was a cold, hard mask. And when he spoke, his voice matched the mask.

'Construction starts in earnest after tomorrow. Right now the men are getting familiar with the island, setting their equipment in place, staking out their sites. Nothing too strenuous. Meals can be light.'

His eyes narrowed on her face and in them she saw the strength and the power that had propelled him to the top...and the ruthlessness that would have no qualms about destroying anyone foolish enough to stand in his way!

'But after tomorrow they must be fed well and fed properly. That means no shortcuts. If you need an assistant, let Max know and she will arrange someone for you.'

'Thank you,' Kelly answered stiffly, matching his cold, impersonal tone. 'But that won't be necessary. I shall do it all myself.'

'Then I suggest you get started. The men will be here shortly for their afternoon tea.'

'Afternoon tea? But they've just finished lunch!' Kelly blurted and immediately cursed her tongue. 'I . . . I shall get started on it right away!' she added quickly.

'Good.' His blue-black eyes swept over her and she felt herself tremble. 'Of course, it goes without saying you won't have time to stand at the door gawking and grinning at people in the compound!'

An embarrassed flush danced across her cheeks. 'I wasn't gawking,' she muttered. 'I was...watching Max.'

'Why?'

'I don't know *why*,' she flared angrily. 'I just was, that's all.'

'Well, Max is sitting behind her desk by now.' He opened the door and stepped outside. 'I suggest you get behind your stove!'

'Right away, Boss,' she answered politely and under her breath silently cursed him. It was almost touching how much better it made her feel.

CHAPTER SIX

BEDLAM reigned in the mess hall. The young workers, most of them apprentices and still in their teens, behaved as if they thought they were at holiday camp. They had stomped into the dining hall, boots and all, straight upon their arrival from their works sites, covered in dust and grime and not smelling very pretty. At afternoon tea they had behaved well, were polite, even exhibiting traces of shyness, but now that they knew Kelly and each other better, they were behaving like a bunch of teenage delinquents, each trying to outdo the other.

They raced between the dining room and the kitchen, knocking over chairs, opening up drawers and cupboards, helping themselves to whatever caught their fancy, ripping apart packets, spilling the contents on the counters, teasing Kelly as she stood sweltering in front of the barbecue, the hot grease from the hamburger patties splattering up and burning her bare arms while she tried to keep track of what they were doing... opening...spilling...begging them to get out of the kitchen, pleading with them to please sit down at the tables. Finally, in desperation, she grabbed a huge pot and banged it loudly several times with a large cooking spoon. The noise was deafening but then it had to be to rise above the din.

'*Get out of this kitchen*!' Kelly roared. '*Right now! Immediately*!' She banged the pot again and glared ferociously around at them. 'If you're not out of this kitchen in ten seconds flat and sitting quietly down at the tables, then this barbecue gets turned off and there will be no dinner served to any of you tonight! And that goes for supper, as well!'

To her astonishment, they quickly vacated the kitchen, hurriedly picked up overturned chairs and started placing them back around the tables before they sat meekly down. Kelly followed them into the dining room, maintaining her fierce expression as she waved the spoon at their bowed heads.

'That's much better. Now, when you've finished eating, you will clean up the mess you made in the kitchen and if any of you ever dares come over here before you hear this gong—' she banged loudly on the pot three times '—then I will put you to work peeling vegetables.' She glared around the tables. 'Is that clear?'

The young workers quickly nodded, keeping their heads bowed. Kelly moved closer to the tables, punctuating each word with a sharp wave of the spoon. 'After tonight, no one eats their evening meal at these tables unless they've showered and dressed cleanly and neatly in casual clothing.' She glared fiercely around the tables. 'Is *that* clear?'

Again they nodded but this time several glanced uneasily towards the door. Kelly followed their eyes. Jack was standing just inside the hall, leaning against the door jamb, eyes narrowed into menacing slits, arms folded across his chest, feet crossed at the ankles. Her cheeks burned a fiery red and she quickly lowered the spoon, wondering how long he had been standing there and realising long enough for the men to have obeyed her orders so quickly.

'Having disciplinary problems, Miss McGuire?' he growled softly and pushed himself away from the door to begin a slow pace around the tables.

Kelly's face continued to burn. 'No, no, everything is under control. Everything's f-fine.'

'The lads behaving themselves, are they?'

'Yes, yes, you can see they are.'

'Good!' He continued his slow pace, his narrowed eyes forcing each young worker to look guiltily up at him. 'Because I won't tolerate unruly behaviour. Any nonsense, either here or on the building site, will result in instant dismissal!'

He raised a black brow and jerked his head towards the kitchen, indicating he wished to speak with her. Kelly meekly followed, her heart filled with despair. She had failed to maintain control. Unlike the young hooligans now sitting like angels at the tables, she very much doubted she would be given a second chance.

Jack looked around at the mess in the kitchen. Kelly's heart sank deeper yet. A cyclone could not have done much better.

'What happened?' he asked softly but there was no mistaking the controlled anger in his voice.

Kelly shook her head and bit her bottom lip, fighting back tears. 'I...I don't honestly know. They...they just seemed to go crazy!'

'They were obviously trying you out.' He gently touched her cheek. 'You're all right?'

'Yes, yes, I'm fine.'

He glanced again at the destruction and then at the pot and spoon she still held in her hand. Suddenly he grinned. 'You did well. I don't think you will have any further trouble.' The grin broadened. 'You even frightened me!'

Kelly sheepishly placed the spoon and pot down onto the counter. 'I guess it was better than firing a gun into the air.'

Jack chuckled. 'Much better.' The amusement faded from his eyes. 'If ever this sort of thing happens again, Kelly, you're not to try to handle it by yourself. You're to report it to me immediately.' He mimicked her ferocious tone. '*Is that clear*?'

Kelly grinned and meekly bowed her head. 'Yes, sir!'

His soft, easy chuckle washed over her, warming her, and when she lifted her eyes to meet his, her heart seemed to jump all the way up to her throat.

'Are you sure you wouldn't want an assistant? At least for the evening meals?'

'No, thank you.' Her eyes swept over the debris. 'I don't think this sort of thing will ever happen again, but if it does, there are thirty pairs of hands who will put it right.'

'But you're not to try to handle it yourself. Remember,' he added warningly, 'you're to report any more nonsense to me.'

'I will,' she promised and, with her heart singing with the praise she had just received, walked with him to the door. His narrowed eyes swept warningly around at the subdued faces before he let himself out. When the door banged shut behind him, there was an immediate, collective sigh of relief from the young apprentices and labourers. Kelly hurried back to the kitchen and loaded the hamburgers onto several large platters and placed them on the tables in front of them.

'There's three whoppers each,' she announced and smiled at their still-solemn faces. 'Cheer up, lads. There's custard tart and ice cream for dessert.' She added brightly, 'You can burn off the calories while you're scrubbing up the kitchen.'

Max came over twice and Jack three times to check that all was going well with the cleaning up. His presence was enough to remind them that a force greater than themselves ruled the island! When Kelly finally finished work that night, she was so exhausted she was actually shaking. She made her way across the moon-drenched compound to her dorm, gathered up her nightie, towel and toiletry bag and headed for the showers. The shower block was hot and damp and there were the lingering odours of soaps, shampoos and toothpaste. Several discarded towels lay draped on benches or on the floor. Kelly picked them up and hung them on wooden pegs stretched along one wall. She selected a stall, removed her·clothing and stepped gratefully under the cool blast of water. When she returned to her room, she wearily made up her bed, turned on the fan, opened the window, set her alarm and lay down.

But she couldn't sleep. She was keyed up by the day, by the unaccustomed work. The muscles in her legs twitched spasmodically from standing on them for almost twelve hours non-stop and her forearms stung from the small burns received from the barbecue. The room was hot and stuffy and even with the window wide open and the fan blowing directly on her, she still couldn't sleep. In desperation, Kelly got up, slipped into her robe and let herself out the door. A few minutes later she was walking slowly along the beach, her feet in the foaming surf. Gradually, she began to unwind and relax. The soft, balmy tropical breeze fanned her hot cheeks, lifted her hair from her shoulders and several times she bent and splashed water onto her burns.

She didn't know the island or the beach. She had simply followed the path down to it and started walking. The palm trees rustled in the ocean breezes and helped soothe her soul. She walked on and on, close to collapsing, but reluctant to return to the close confines of her room, wishing she could stretch out on the soft sand, shut her eyes and go to sleep.

A small inlet appeared suddenly in front of her, closing off the stretch of beach. The waters were calm, not a ripple, protected from the ocean breezes by a circle of coconut palms. A single rock, a metre high and polished a silver grey from the endless surge of the surf, jutted out from the water and onto the powdery white sand. Kelly climbed onto it. It felt warm and smooth under her bare feet. She removed her robe and her nightie, placed them in a small bundle by her feet, stood for several moments on the edge of the rock, the soft tropical breezes caressing her beautiful, slender body before she slowly lowered herself into the water.

'I'd join you...but I just got out!'

At first Kelly imagined she had heard a voice, *his* voice, that her poor exhausted mind was simply playing tricks on her. She quickly pushed her hair out of her eyes and blinked across the small inlet to the other side, her eyes widening at the sight of Jack standing wet and naked on the soft sand, his teeth gleaming white in his tanned face as he slowly grinned and just as slowly wrapped a towel around his trim waist, knotting it at the side. He circled the tiny inlet and stood gazing down at her, his midnight blue eyes as bewitching as his smile.

'Ah, it's only you, Kelly. I thought it must be a mermaid!'

'Not funny.' She pointed stiffly to her nightclothes on the rock by his feet. 'Would you pass me my robe, please?'

He looked down at the small, neat bundle and squatted comfortably beside it. 'You don't want your robe yet,' he growled purringly. 'You just got in.'

'I do want it.'

His grin broadened and he shook his dark, wet head. 'Don't be silly. You walked all this way for a swim in my cove and—'

Kelly gasped. 'Your cove?' She gaped disbelievingly up at him. 'This…this is your cove?' And over his broad shoulder she saw the small veranda of his van splashed with the silvery light of the moon.

He laughed softly. 'You know damned well it is.' His eyes gleamed down at her. 'And I want you to have that swim. In fact, I insist upon it. After all, you've had a rough day.' He leaned comfortably back on the rock, supported by his elbows. 'I'll even watch you, make certain you come to no harm.'

'I don't want you to watch me.'

'Sure you do. Otherwise, you wouldn't have come!'

Kelly couldn't believe the conceit of the man. 'I had no idea I would find you here.' Her cheeks reddened at his disbelieving smile. 'Well, I didn't! How would I, when this is the first time I've been on the beach? Max took me to your van by Jeep…through…through a tangled, overgrown track.' She added desperately, 'If you must know, the only reason I decided on a walk at all was…was because I couldn't sleep…'

'Alone. I know.' He nodded in sympathy. 'That sometimes happens to me, too.' He stretched out his hand. 'All right,' he sighed. 'You can sleep with me.'

Kelly ignored the interruption, his outstretched hand *and* most especially his outrageous invitation. 'I couldn't sleep,' she continued tersely, 'because I was *too tired* to sleep. I gave up trying and thought a...a walk on the beach might help...might help me to relax.'

'Walks are good,' he solemnly agreed. 'But there are other more effective ways of relaxing!'

'Yes, and I'm sure you know them all!'

'Well, I try to keep up with the latest methods.'

'How sporting of you.' She found herself being caught up in the dark, mysterious depths of his eyes and hastily looked away. 'Now...now would you please hand me my robe,' she added desperately.

'You're quite certain you don't want a swim?'

'Quite certain,' Kelly answered stiffly.

'Would you change your mind if I joined you?' And to her horror he stood up and started to untie the towel at his waist.

'I most definitely would not change my mind...and don't you dare remove that towel!' she added shakily. 'Now...now would you please hand me my robe.'

He picked up the bundle, separated the robe from the nightie and handed it to her. When she reached for it, he took her hand and pulled her swiftly to her feet. Water formed tiny rivulets down her beautiful, glistening body.

'You beast!' she yelped and grabbed her robe.

He chuckled softly but it ended swiftly when he noticed for the first time the tiny burn marks scattered across her arms. 'What are these?' he demanded to know.

'N-Nothing! They're nothing.' She quickly slipped into her robe and tied it snugly around her slender waist.

Jack grabbed her wrists and, despite her protests, forced the sleeves up. 'Burns!' he exclaimed. 'Hundreds of them!' He looked at her in alarm. 'How did this happen?'

'While I was cooking the hamburgers.' She pulled down her sleeves and stuck her hands into her pockets.

'What have you done about them?'

She shrugged her small shoulders. 'Nothing.'

'Nothing!' he exploded. 'Burns are easily infected.'

'They're only small.'

He looked at her in exasperation. 'Good grief, Kelly, are you really that stupid? Even the tiniest of scratches can become seriously infected in a matter of hours in the tropics.' Jack pulled her hands out of her pockets and again rolled up her sleeves, bending his head as he carefully examined her arms, his fingers gentle on her injured skin. 'You're lucky! The blisters aren't broken and there's no immediate sign of infection.' He rolled down her sleeves. 'But that won't last.' He gripped her firmly under the elbow. 'I've got a first-aid kit in the van. You're coming with me.'

Kelly drew back in alarm. 'No!' Panic filled her eyes. 'I'll visit the infirmary in the morning. I promise! First thing,' she added desperately, her earlier visit to his van etched all too painfully clearly in her mind.

'Nonsense! Those burns need tending to now!' He bent down, swooped up her nightie, tucked it under his arm and, ignoring her protests, led her up a small narrow path to his van. Once inside, he switched on the lights and Kelly took a swift, uneasy glance around. His dinner dishes had been washed and lay in a drying rack by the sink. It seemed a lonesome sight, the single plate, glass, cup, knife and fork. Jack walked immediately over to a cupboard and pulled out a gleaming black box, presumably the first-aid kit.

'Take off your robe,' he ordered curtly.

Kelly's hands flew protectively to the knotted sash. 'I most certainly will not!'

A look of annoyance flashed across his eyes. 'I need to have a closer look at those burns... and I can't very well apply the cream through the material of your robe.'

'I can apply the cream.' She held out a shaking hand. 'Back in my dorm.'

'You could,' he agreed, 'but I'd feel much better if I did it. That way, I will sleep soundly—' his eyes gleamed down at her '—knowing I've taken care of you.'

'I can take care of myself!'

'Obviously not as well as you might... otherwise we wouldn't be having this conversation!' He sighed heavily, and for the first time Kelly noticed how tired he looked. Her day had been long and hard and, obviously, so had his.

'You... you took my nightie. I haven't anything on under my robe.'

'Your nightie is right there on that chair beside you.' He picked it up and handed it to her. 'Go into my bedroom. You can put it on there.'

Kelly hurried into the bedroom, deliberately ignored the huge king-size bed, pulled off her robe, slipped into her sleeveless white cotton nightie, put the robe on again. When she returned to the kitchen, Jack had slipped into a robe of his own, black silk, tied loosely around his waist, making him look far more sexy than should ever be decently allowed! He had pulled out two chairs, facing each other.

'Sit,' he commanded. 'And for Pete's sake, take off that robe.'

Kelly nervously removed it, sat gingerly down on the edge of the chair and folded it neatly across her lap. Jack sat down, the tube of antiseptic burn cream in one huge, strong brown hand. Kelly shivered and squeezed her eyes shut when he reached for her hands and rested her arms across his hard, muscular thighs. She held her breath as she felt the cool, soothing cream being applied evenly and gently across her injured skin, and the palms of her hands trembled and burned into the silk covering his thighs.

'There,' he announced gruffly. 'You can open your eyes now, Kelly. It's all done.'

Kelly slowly pried her eyes open and looked down at her pale, slender arms stretched across his lap. 'Are you sure...?' She ran the tip of her small tongue across her lips. 'Are you sure...I don't need some more?'

'Quite sure.' He picked up her hands and pressed the palms to his lips, his eyes holding hers. A roaring filled her ears and her throat went suddenly dry. 'I'll drive you back to your dorm.'

He stood up abruptly, placed the cap back on the tube and tucked it into the pocket of her robe, before reaching down and pulling her gently to her feet. Kelly blinked as if she had suddenly awakened and didn't quite know where she was. He helped her on with her robe and told her to apply fresh cream to her burns in the morning. She nodded as if she actually understood what he was saying. It wasn't until she was standing next to him by the Jeep that she finally regained control of herself. She stepped abruptly back and looked up at him with alarm.

'You can't drive me back. S-Someone might see us or... hear the motor.'

He shrugged his massive shoulders. 'I doubt it but what if they do?'

Her beautiful green eyes widened. 'We're both in our dressing gowns!'

He chuckled softly. 'And people might get the wrong impression?'

'Well, yes...!'

'Very well.' He smiled down at her and traced the outline of her soft cheek. 'I'll walk you back along the beach.'

'It's...' She swallowed hard, her heart racing. 'It's not necessary.'

'Yes... it is.'

They walked in almost total silence back to the path leading up to the camp. The moon lit up the beach and it was as if they were walking on a soft, silvery blanket. There was no awkwardness, just a companionable silence, and while he didn't make any attempt to hold her hand, sometimes their hands would touch or their fingers would brush together. At the edge of the path, they stopped, and Kelly looked up at him, the stars above reflected in her eyes. She moved slightly closer to him, her lips parted, shamelessly inviting his kiss.

'Good night,' she whispered and the thumping of her heart was mercifully drowned by the pounding of the sea charging across the silvery shores.

'Good night.' He bent his dark head and kissed her lightly on the cheek. 'Take care of those burns.'

And then he turned and left her there...and as she watched his proud, broad shoulders disappearing down the moon-drenched beach, she felt tears roll down her cheeks. She lifted her hand...and touched where he had kissed her.

CHAPTER SEVEN

IT WAS one hundred and eight degrees in the shade but Kelly hardly seemed to notice. Her hair was tucked under her old straw hat and she wore a white sleeveless T-shirt and a pair of faded blue-jean shorts. She had kicked off her sandals and was happily planting petunias in a small garden bed she had prepared outside the kitchen window. The punnets of petunias had been ordered along with her usual kitchen supplies and had arrived by barge yesterday morning. Kelly had kept them hidden in her room until today, when Jack was in Sydney where he would be for the remainder of the week. She wanted to surprise him and, of course, hopefully the flowers would remind him of his promise!

She hummed softly and for a short while was able to forget the exhausting routine of the kitchen, the never-ending sameness of chores. She was bored with cooking the same old meals: steaks, chops, roasts and stews with the usual mountains of potatoes and vegetables. Once she had spent the day marinating cubes of beef, patiently skewering them onto one hundred and twenty bamboo sticks with chunks of onion, tomato and capsicum nestled in between. The kebabs were served on beds of steamed rice with side salads. The men were delighted and devoured them in minutes. When they looked at her expectantly, her heart sank. They thought she had simply served them up a tasty little appetiser! She told them that was it, that was their meal. They immediately picked up their spoons, banged them on the table and chanted, 'We want *food*! We want *food*!' After that, she had wisely stuck to the steaks, chops, roasts and stews.

She felt chained to the sink and stove, confined between four walls, the daily trek from the dorm to the kitchen and back again her only time spent outdoors. She sorely missed her *real* work. Missed the creativity. Missed the challenge and excitement of taking a drab piece of landscape and turning it into something beautiful. Missed seeing the joy in her clients' eyes when they saw what she had created for them. At night, when she lay in bed so exhausted she could barely move, she would think of Jack's promise and it was enough to keep her going.

'What on earth is all of this?' a deep voice above her growled.

Kelly looked up quickly from her small garden, a tiny seedling suspended in her hand. Jack peered down at her, a disapproving scowl darkening his handsome features. He was dressed in cream-coloured slacks and a deep blue short-sleeved silk shirt, the colour almost as vibrant as his eyes. Kelly jumped guiltily to her feet and brushed the soil from the knees of her bare legs.

'Why aren't you in Sydney?' she blurted.

His eyes narrowed. 'Aha! I thought as much. While the cat's away the mouse will play, huh?'

A dark flush rose swiftly to her cheeks. 'This isn't *playing*!' Kelly stated indignantly. 'I'm simply trying to make my work environment more pleasant.' She swallowed hard, fearful he might order her to stop work on her garden, order her to abandon it altogether. 'I . . . I need to have something pretty, something bright and cheerful to look at.'

'Something *pretty* to look at?' he repeated incredulously. 'Good grief, woman, look around. You happen to be on one of the prettiest islands in the world. Most people would give their eye-teeth to be surrounded by such magnificent beauty.'

'I...I know but...but I can't see any of it from the kitchen window. I can only see the compound and it always looks the same, so hot and dusty.'

He considered her words for several heart-stopping seconds before peering down at the seedlings. 'How do you propose to water this...this new environment?' His eyes returned to her face. 'Or hadn't you thought of that?'

Until the huge underground storage tanks were installed, the camp relied entirely on rainwater collected in tanks. There were reminders everywhere to conserve its usage. Kelly knew it would be unthinkable that such a precious commodity be used to water her garden.

'Dishwater,' she answered promptly. 'I plan to use leftover dishwater.'

Jack stared at her. '*Dish*water?'

Kelly chuckled. 'Don't look so horrified. The soap is biodegradable and won't harm the plants. In fact, it will do them good, help nourish them.'

He rubbed his chin and peered again at the little garden. 'Well, it certainly appears you've thought of everything,' he drawled. 'Even waited until you thought I'd gone!'

Kelly stared down at her bare feet, feeling guilty and not just a little foolish.

'Did you really think I would deny you the pleasure of a few simple flowers, Kelly?' he added softly.

Kelly looked helplessly up at him. She wanted desperately to tell him the real reason she had started the garden but something held her back. Maybe it was the fear of hearing he had reconsidered his promise, that he had thought about it and decided she wouldn't be suitable for one of his gardening projects after all. The promise was what kept her going, what kept her chained to the sink and stove. Without it...

'I...I...'

'Well, *did* you?'

She nodded, feeling miserable. 'Yes,' she whispered.

His mouth tightened. 'I see.' He sighed heavily. 'Well, at least you didn't think I would make you remove them once they had established themselves!'

Kelly watched him march stiffly across the compound to a waiting Jeep. When he opened the door, she could see his briefcase on the passenger seat and his suitcase on the floor. There was a cloud of dust as he roared off in the direction of the airstrip. She was still standing in her little garden when the *Jabiru* flew overhead. She raised her hand to shield her eyes from the hot, glaring sun but it was her sudden rush of tears and not the sun that blurred the tiny aircraft from her vision.

When Jack flew over the compound ten days later, he fully expected to see Kelly's garden in full bloom. What he didn't expect were several more gardens, also in full bloom! He couldn't believe his eyes when he saw one of his crusty old engineers diligently pulling weeds from the garden in front of his van and, good heavens, there was Max, happily scooping out water from a dish pan onto her own little bed of flowers. Jack shook his head and grinned. Kelly had certainly spruced up the place. She was a virtual little Johnny Appleseed!

Kelly's heart skipped several beats when she heard the *Jabiru* fly over the camp just as she was opening the door to the oven to check on the three huge roasts of beef. They were almost done. She cast an anxious eye at the wall clock. Five-fifteen. Forty-five minutes until the men pushed their way into the dining hall. She closed the oven door and opened the next one. The potatoes and chunks of pumpkin were browning nicely on their long, flat trays. She adjusted the temperature so they wouldn't get too dark and inspected the big pots on top of the stove. The water covering the carrots and turnips had barely started to boil. She lowered the heat to simmer so they wouldn't overcook. It wouldn't do to be accused of serving mushy vegetables!

The bowls had already been placed in the warming closet of the oven, and even though the tables in the dining room were set, Kelly checked on them again. The men ate breakfast, lunch, morning and afternoon teas from bare tables but Kelly had decided their evening meals should be special. She had found a drawer filled with oversize aprons and bright tablecloths and tonight the tables looked particularly festive with their vibrant red cloths beneath gleaming white crockery, sparkling cutlery and small bowls of delicate petunias picked from her garden. Whenever Max had travelled to the mainland, Kelly had her pick up huge travel posters, which now entirely covered the fabricated walls. The harsh overhead light bulbs had been replaced with soft pink-tinged globes. The whole effect was warm and cosy. If Jack walked in right now, Kelly thought proudly, he could easily be forgiven for thinking he had stepped straight into, well, maybe not the Waldorf, but something pretty special.

Not that she expected him to walk right in, of course. She knew he would consult with Max and his engineers and architects as he always did after he had been away for any considerable length of time and then head straight for his van, tired from his business trip. But maybe... maybe tonight he might pop in and say something nice about all the flowers she had planted around the compound. Everyone loved them and it gave them something to do in the cool of the mornings and early evenings, a sort-of hobby. She leaned across the table and gently touched one of the petunias, her expression soft and dreamy. Sometimes Jack flew across to Airlie Beach, the main resort area on the Whitsunday coast. Max said he owned a house there and Kelly often found herself wondering what it was like and now... now she found herself wondering if he had any gardens.

With a heavy sigh, Kelly pushed Jack firmly out of her thoughts and returned to the overwhelming heat of the kitchen. Cooking is the easy part, she decided. Timing was something else again. Each meal was a challenge. But she was getting better and better at it. Tonight, she had carefully estimated it would take approximately twenty minutes to make the gravy, carve the roasts with the electric knife, remove the potatoes and vegetables from their pots and pans, place them into the bowls and carry everything into the dining room. She lifted the hem of her long apron, which fell well below her yellow one-piece sun-suit, and wiped the perspiration from her face and neck. Even her undergarments felt damp and clung uncomfortably to her skin.

According to her well-planned schedule, now was the time to get the apple pies from the freezer and place them into the oven. They would cook quite nicely in the reduced heat and be ready by the time the men had finished their main course. Kelly pushed open the heavy door of the freezer. The immediate rush of cold air felt delicious as it drifted over her heated skin. She switched on the light, but when she started to step inside and even though she had already made hundreds of excursions into the huge vault, she suddenly felt extremely wary.

What if the door slammed shut and she was unable to escape? No one would know she was there, trapped, until they came looking for their dinner.

And that wouldn't be until six o'clock! Was it possible to freeze to death in forty-five minutes? she nervously wondered as she lingered uneasily by the door. Maybe not, but she would at least receive a bad case of frostbite. The very thought of being locked up anywhere, unable to escape, was horrible enough, but to be trapped inside a freezer, slowly stiffening into a block of ice, was absolutely terrifying.

She frantically hunted around for something suitable and trustworthy to keep the door wide open while she was in there and finally settled on a broom. She jammed one end snugly under the lock and the other end firmly into the groove where the door rested when it was closed. Satisfied as she could possibly be with this unlikely safety measure, Kelly cautiously entered the freezer vault.

The icy blast took her breath away as she flew over to the section where the various sweets were stored, quickly loaded her arms with a dozen pies, ran back with them into the kitchen, dumped them onto the stainless-steel counter and breathed a huge sigh of relief.

'Good grief, woman! Are you out of your mind?'

Kelly whirled with a start at the sound of the harshly accusing voice. Through the frosty vapours billowing majestically from the freezer vault into the hot, steamy kitchen, she could see the tall, dark, imposing figure of Jack, dressed in a green short-sleeved shirt and chocolate brown trousers, standing in the doorway. Kelly's heart skittered crazily across her chest. He had obviously come straight from the airstrip, stopping to see her first before any of the others. He stormed through the clouds, knocked away the broom and slammed the freezer door shut.

'I can't believe you could be so irresponsible! Using the freezer as a . . . as an *air-conditioner*!'

'I wasn't. I—'

'How long have you had that door open?' he bellowed.

'Not long, just—'

'*Quiet!*' He held up a restraining hand, his head cocked to one side as he listened intently to the sound of the motor. Kelly held her breath as she listened, too.

'Sounds all right to me,' she said with a confident nod after several tense seconds had slowly passed.

Fresh anger blazed in his eyes as he stared at her, hardly believing her audacity. 'Does it now?' His voice was laced with sarcasm. 'How reassuring. And what would you happen to know about motors?'

'Quite a lot, actually,' she answered stiffly, infuriated by his tone. 'You haven't forgotten, have you, that I once had my own business, with my own machinery?'

'Then you should know that by leaving the door open, you're forcing the motor to work overtime, non-stop, eventually burning it out!' Fury danced in his eyes. 'How long do you think the food would keep in this heat? How could you be so *stupid*? So *careless*?'

Tears of hurt and frustration stung her eyes. 'Why don't you just sack me and get it done with?' A broken sob tore from her throat. 'You don't want me here. You never did. You only hired me to ease your guilty conscience!'

The anger drained from him as quickly as it had risen. He dragged a hand wearily through his hair. 'Forget about being sacked, Kelly. That would be far too easy. For both of us!'

'Well,' she sniffed, turning quickly away from him and wiping viciously at her eyes with the corner of her monstrous apron, 'd-don't think I'm going to make things any easier by qu-quitting!'

Jack could see the quivering of her small shoulders and hear her muffled sobs as she tried to conceal her emotions. The backs of her long, slender legs were barely visible through the opening of the back of the apron. Where had she got such a thing? He jammed his hands into the pockets of his trousers, annoyed with himself for coming into the kitchen and even more so for wanting now to take her into his arms and comfort her. He shook his dark head. She had placed the motor in jeopardy and he wanted to *comfort* her? The cheerful humming of the freezer cut through the oppressive heat of the kitchen and was oddly out of tune with her muffled sobs.

'I...I was afraid,' she suddenly whispered.

'What?' Jack placed his hands on her shoulders and turned her gently around, his black brows drawn into a disbelieving frown as he searched her tear-streaked face.

Kelly bit her bottom lip and added in a small, defensive voice, 'It sounds silly, I know, especially when I've been going in and out of it all along but...' Her eyes darted fearfully towards the freezer and she added in a whisper as though terrified it might hear and actually do it, 'What if the door gets stuck and . . . and I'm trapped inside?'

'That's why you left the door open?' he asked hoarsely.

Kelly nodded and dragged her eyes up to meet his, her hands nervously twisting the long sash of her apron, which had been wrapped twice around her small waist and fastened in a bow just below her heart. 'It was only for a moment. Two at the very most. I was getting out the pies.' She quickly indicated them on the counter. 'I used the broom to keep the door open only while I was inside. I was going to remove it straightaway but you came in and . . . and did it for me!'

A dark flush spread across his hard cheeks. 'Yes, I certainly did that!' He shook his head in exasperation. 'Why didn't you just *say* you were afraid?' He cradled her face in his hands and gently wiped away her tears with his thumbs. 'Why make us go through all this . . . all this unpleasantness?'

'You didn't give me a chance,' she said in a small voice.

'No,' he sighed. 'I guess I didn't. But that's mainly because you seem to take advantage of chances! How is it your one small garden has managed to spread itself across the entire compound?'

Kelly peeped cautiously up at him through the long, silky fringe of her lashes. Despite the tone of his voice, she realized with a burst of joy that he didn't seem to mind in the least. The corners of her mouth lifted in a smile. 'Gardens have a way of doing that,' she answered with a simple honesty, her bright, clear green eyes holding his. 'They like to spread their happiness,' she added huskily.

For several seconds, Jack gazed down at her as though trapped in her spell. Then he smiled, took her small hand in his, led her over to the freezer vault and indicated the inner and outer locks on the heavy door. 'Designed for safety. You can unlock the door from the inside just as easily as you can from the outside. There's nothing to fear.'

'You're quite sure?' Kelly hedged, uneasiness creeping back into her voice.

'Quite sure.' He demonstrated for her and patiently had her do the same several times in order to reassure her.

'What if the light burns out when I'm inside and I can't find my way back to the door?' she asked fearfully as this new possibility struck her.

'The light is battery operated, good for three years. And the battery is brand new,' he added, anticipating her next question.

'But it could be faulty!'

'It was tested before it was installed.'

'What if the inside lock got *stuck*?'

'I've never known it to happen.'

'Never known...!' Her eyes widened in terror. 'But it *could* happen? Is that what you're *saying*?'

'I'm saying I've never known it to happen and I haven't.' His tone told her his patience was wearing thin. 'I've been using this type of freezer on construction sites for years. There's never been a single mishap.'

'Mishap!' She shuddered. 'Freezing to death could hardly be considered a *mishap*!'

'Actually, they say it's not an entirely bad way to go!' He slammed the freezer door shut. 'Where's your protective clothing?'

'Protective clothing?' Kelly ran her hands hesitantly down her apron. 'You mean . . . this?'

'Of course not!' His dark blue eyes quickly scanned the room. 'Your coat. Hat. Boots.'

'I'm to wear such things in *here*?' she asked, totally dismayed.

'Don't be ridiculous!' Her cheeks flamed at the look he gave her. 'You're to wear such things in the freezer vault! It's a simple precaution. No wonder you're feeling edgy. You've been exposing yourself to extremes in temperature.'

Kelly chewed on her bottom lip. She should have realized what was happening and taken the simple precaution herself . . . *without* having to be told! How could she expect him to consider her future jobs if she proved herself careless or inadequate in this one?

'I didn't bring anything like that with me,' she admitted guiltily, feeling overwhelmed by her despair.

'Max will fix you up with the necessary gear.'

Kelly nodded and lowered her eyes, too distressed to speak. She felt all her hard work over the past several weeks was going down the drain. What she didn't see was the quick flash of amusement in his eyes. 'Cut the act, Kelly!'

Her eyes flew up to his face. 'Act?'

'Pretending to be the humble maiden. The dutiful slave. It doesn't suit you.'

Her eyes widened in astonishment. 'I . . . I *wasn't—*'

'And tell Max to get you some decent-fitting aprons. You look like an urchin in that one.'

Red-hot flames lapped at her cheeks. 'I thought you liked humble and dutiful.'

'Not in you, I don't.' His blue eyes gleamed and deepened to indigo as they took hold of hers. 'On you, it's not . . . natural!'

'I can be humble,' she flared. 'And dutiful, too!'

He grinned. '*That* we shall have to see!'

'But you've already seen! What could possibly be more humble than slaving over a hot stove in this heat? That's not only *humble*, it's downright *dutiful*!'

'It's neither!' he returned crisply. 'It's simply your job!'

'A humbling job, nonetheless!'

His eyes hardened. 'It's a job you're lucky to have!'

Kelly struggled to control her fury. 'For your information, Jack Saunders, you were right the first time. I *was* pretending to be humble. *Pretending*. Nothing you could say or do to me could ever make me feel humble.' Her voice rose dramatically. 'I'll gladly peel a hundred sacks of potatoes, wash a thousand dishes, scrub pots, sleep in a makeshift dorm and still not be humbled. And do you want to know why?' she cried fiercely.

'I can hardly wait to be told,' he answered drily.

'Because I'm a survivor!' Her eyes blazed with triumph.

A wicked gleam danced in his eyes. 'There's still a long road ahead!'

His chiding tone only fuelled her anger. Her green eyes clawed at him like talons as she watched him go over to the sink and casually pour himself a glass of water. Despite the heat of the kitchen, there wasn't a drop of per-

spiration on the hard, lean length of his body. He raised
the glass to his lips, his strong, tanned fingers wrapped
around the vessel, biceps bulging and straining against
the green fabric of his silk shirt with the action. He drank
several glasses and while he drank she continued to
watch, at first because she was hoping he would choke,
and then because she had become spellbound, totally in
awe of him.

The kitchen was large, huge, the ceiling high, but even
so, his presence seemed to fill the entire space, sucking
up the oxygen, making it hotter, stiller. The atmosphere
became charged with strange rippling currents. Mysterious forces reached out for her, making her feel quite
weak, defenceless, and she was drawn once again into
his strange mystical power, his absolute control.

He sensed the effect he was having on her, slowly put
the glass down on the counter and, just as slowly, turned
to look at her. She watched, mesmerised, totally en-
tranced as he dragged his hand roughly across his mouth,
his eyes entrapping her own. He reached out, ran his
finger along her cheek and across her trembling lips,
down the side of her neck, across one small breast and
down to the bow tied beneath her pounding heart. A
spurt of hungry desire spiralled throughout her body,
shocking and shaming her, and incredulously she could
actually feel the answering, raging heat from his own
body, setting her thighs and groin on fire. Her body
tensed, waited, the anticipation becoming unbearable.

The smouldering flames in his eyes grew irresistibly
brighter, drawing her into their force. His hand slipped
under the bow, drawing her closer. With a cry of sur-
render, Kelly raised her slender arms and wrapped them
around his neck, her fingers digging into his thick, wiry

hair, her soft thighs pressing eagerly against the steel power of his own. His mouth covered hers, hot and demanding, and she returned his kiss with the same fiery passion. He crushed her against him, his hands caressing the length of her back, pressing her hips against his, and she felt her body melting and blending with his own. The gasp that tore from her throat was the sweetest of all agonies and the flames of their desire rocked their bodies.

A pot boiled over on the stove followed quickly by the acrid stench of scorched vegetables. Jack was quick to react. He set Kelly away from him and, in the same swift movement, rescued the burning pot and switched off the gas.

Shaken, Kelly grabbed a cloth and frantically began mopping up the dreadful mess on the stove. Her small shoulder accidentally brushed against his and she reared back guiltily, her cheeks burning with shame. But Jack appeared not to notice. He calmly poured the contents of the charred pot into a bowl.

How can he pretend nothing has happened? Kelly thought wretchedly. How can he behave as though their actions hadn't almost caused the demise of the meal? She picked up the bowl to place it in the warming closet.

'Oh, no!' she gasped. 'I can't serve these. *Look* at them! They're black, scorched!' Hysteria rose within her. 'Surely you don't expect the men to eat *scorched* carrots!'

'Of course not.' He grabbed a towel and wiped his hands. 'You will need to prepare them some more!'

His words and the autocratic tone in which they were delivered filled her with a cold rage. Her hands trembled as she placed the bowl back onto the counter. 'None of this would have happened if you hadn't come in here,' she stated icily.

'Probably not!' He folded the towel and calmly placed it back on its rack.

Kelly's fury sky-rocketed. 'I don't want you in my kitchen! I don't want you interfering with my job. I don't want you anywhere near me!' She pummelled the hard, broad wall of his chest with her small fists. 'Do you hear me?' she cried. 'I want you to stay *away* from me!'

He grabbed both of her hands into one of his, a dark censor in his eyes. 'You're lying, Kelly McGuire.' His other hand curved around her flushed cheek and he smiled. 'Your eyes are the colour of a rich green moss!'

He released her abruptly and shoved his hands into the pockets of his jeans. 'But you're absolutely right! No one should unnecessarily interfere with another person's work. I expect you to remember that! However, I make it a rule to check on my employees to see how they're getting along and eliminate any problems or difficulties they might be experiencing during their first few weeks on the job. A perfect example of that would be your concerns with the freezer.' He raised his arrogant black brows. 'Wouldn't you agree?'

'I . . .' Her gaze faltered and she shook her head helplessly, feeling ridiculously hurt now that she knew his only purpose in visiting her was in his caring role as the 'firm but fair' boss.

'Well?' he prompted softly.

'I agree,' she whispered and her eyes dropped to stare miserably down at the toes of her canvas shoes.

'Good.' She heard the satisfaction in his voice. 'Now, unless you have any further problems, I have other work to do,' he stated impatiently as though she had wasted enough of his time.

'I...I have no further problems,' she muttered and wondered what he would say if she told him her biggest problem was in dealing with him and avoiding the powerful attraction she felt for him!

'Then I shall be on my way.' His eyes lingered on the fiery auburn crown of her bowed head and the stern line of his mouth softened. 'By the way...that meal smells delicious!'

It was the tone as much as the words that filled her with a desperate longing, a need, a fatal urge to call him back! She wanted to thank him for his patience in helping her with her problem, eliminating her fears. She wanted to *feed* him! She knew he wouldn't sit down with the younger men but surely he would appreciate a tray to take back to his lonely van. It wasn't right that he should have to prepare his own meal after having been away for so long. Even without the carrots, there was so much food here. Food she had carefully prepared herself. Food he said...smelled delicious.

'Jack! Wait!' She ran after him, lifting up the hem of her long apron to keep herself from tripping, catching up with him as he was about to step out to the compound. 'I was wondering if...'

She gazed helplessly up at him, galvanised by the eyes that gazed down at her, trapped by the intoxicating, musky male scent that enveloped her. She ran the tip of her pink tongue nervously across her lips.

'I was wondering...' And she knew she couldn't, mustn't, do it. Could not, must not ask if she could perform this simple task for him. It was far too intimate! Too caring! Too thoughtful! Therefore, far too *dangerous*!

He might read something into it, she thought anxiously. Something that wasn't written. Could never be written. The combination of the heat in the kitchen and the frost in the freezer had obviously made her brain go soft. How could she have forgotten, even for a minute, that this man had destroyed everything she had worked for? She didn't care if he had to prepare his own meal. She didn't care if he starved to death! Even the mere thought of what she had been about to do filled her with a wild panic. Her throat grew uncomfortably dry and she had to swallow several times before she trusted herself to continue.

'I was wondering about... about those carrots. Did you really mean it when you said I should prepare some more?'

'Of course I meant it!'

She welcomed his arrogant tone. It made her feel glad, gleeful even, that she hadn't offered to fix him a meal. Thank goodness she had recovered from her strange condition just in the nick of time.

She poked him playfully on the arm. 'The firm but fair boss has spoken, huh?'

The sudden narrowing of his eyes told her he was not amused. But she didn't care. She had saved herself from something far more disastrous than his mere disapproval. She dearly wished she could tell him about her soul-saving victory but that would be *bragging*, she thought gloatingly.

'What are you up to, Kelly?' he asked softly and something in his voice effectively destroyed her fragile euphoria.

'Nothing,' she answered quickly. 'I just wanted to double-check with you. I want to do things properly and ... and you're always so busy that I don't very often get a chance to speak with you, to see if I'm on the right track.'

His black, arrogant brows arched sharply above narrowed eyes. He placed his hands on her shoulders. 'Relax, Kelly, you're doing just fine.' His hands slipped slowly down her arms to her own hands, making her sensitive skin tingle. 'The camp is fast becoming a small community. Pretty soon the "bush telegraph" will be in full swing. Everyone will know what everyone else is doing.' He released her hands but his eyes held her own as his voice became softly intimate. 'I might be kilometres away on the other side of the island but I will know what you served the men for breakfast, lunch and dinner. I will hear what you wore, what you said, how you said it. There's very little I won't know about, Kelly.'

She rubbed her hands over the tingling sensation she could still feel in her arms. 'I ... I guess that can be a good thing,' she answered breathlessly. 'In case I ... *anyone* ... should ever need you,' she quickly corrected herself.

'In case you should ever need me!' he solemnly agreed and her heart somersaulted at the enigmatic gleam in his dark blue eyes.

How could she hate him one minute and like him the next? she frantically asked herself. And then, to her horror, her lips parted and the very words she had fervently vowed she would never speak, tumbled eagerly from her mouth.

'Would you like me to fix you a tray to take back to your van?'

If he was surprised by her offer he didn't show it. 'Thanks, but no. I've got a dinner engagement tonight at one of the island resorts,' he explained.

Her face paled. 'A . . . a dinner engagement?' A *date*?

He nodded. 'With two of my architects.' He glanced at his watch and his black brows arched in surprise. 'In exactly one hour! Which means I must rush.'

Two of his architects. Kelly felt giddy with relief. His architects were all men. 'Yes, well, that's the darnedest thing about being the boss,' she laughed shakily. 'The work is never done.'

He smiled and touched her cheek. 'True,' he agreed.

The men were halfway through their meal when Kelly heard the *Jabiru* fly over the island and knew Jack was on his way. She glanced out the window and was alarmed at how black the tropical night had become. He was obviously an experienced pilot but she shivered at the thought of his flying alone across the fathomless dark sea.

Max came in while she was serving dessert to drop off the white, cotton-lined rubber coat, hat and boots she was to wear in the vault along with some better-fitting aprons. They chatted for a while, mainly about Max's garden, which the older woman had become totally besotted with.

As Kelly cleared the tables, washed the dishes, scrubbed the pots and mopped the floors she paused more than once to think about Jack and the electrifying moments spent in his arms! Then, angry with herself and blushing furiously she would attempt to shove these images to the back of her mind by wondering instead what he and his architects were discussing.

She leaned on her mop and pictured the men, one of them tall, dark and ruggedly handsome with deep cobalt blue eyes, perhaps having drinks at a bar before going into the dining room for dinner, their rolled-up blueprints tucked under their arms the way Jack did around the compound. She wondered what was on the menu and what he would order, and even though the fare would obviously be far more sumptuous and elaborate than what she had prepared, she was overwhelmingly happy that she had offered to fix him a tray. She knew ... she *knew* her simple gesture had pleased him!

At nine o'clock, Kelly laid out a light supper for the men, cleaned up again and by ten o'clock her chores were finally done. She was exhausted, but instead of retiring to her room in the dorm, decided to set the tables for breakfast. That would save time in the morning, she told herself and once again glanced anxiously out the window at the threatening sky.

With the tables set, Kelly looked for other ways to save time, wondering why she had never thought to do this before. She made up pitchers of orange juice, placed them in the refrigerator, took several loaves of bread from the freezer and lined them across the counter to thaw. A box of oatmeal was placed in a handy position by the stove and an enormous pot was filled with water, covered and set in readiness on the unlit burner. Trays of bacon and bowls of eggs were moved to a forward position in the fridge. Apart from actually cooking the breakfast, there wasn't much more she could do!

Except rearrange the pantry shelves, a chore she had planned doing since her very first day on the job but had simply not found the time. It was extremely frustrating searching for items, such as spices, which would be better grouped together instead of scattered helter-skelter on various shelves. Once the pantry was organised to her complete satisfaction, Kelly sat down on a stool at the counter and browsed through the recipe books Max had given her, staring bleary-eyed down at the glossy pages, only her ears alert.

The *Jabiru* touched down quietly just a little before midnight. Kelly heard it plainly along with the sound of a Jeep's motor a few minutes later. Her relief was enormous. She rose from the stool, stretched her tired muscles, tucked the books into a corner of the counter, closed and locked all the windows in the kitchen and dining room, checked to make certain everything was switched off that should be switched off and opened the door just as the Jeep pulled up and Jack leapt out.

Her heart stood still at the sight of him. It was almost like in her dream only instead of a tuxedo he was dressed in a white dinner jacket, white shirt and black slacks. The shirt was unbuttoned at the strong brown column of his neck, the black tie loosened. The soft sea breeze picked up his hair and tossed it slightly back from his brow. Her throat tightened at the incredibly handsome picture he made, standing there so tall and elegant, his midnight blue eyes holding the clear, unblinking green of her own in her small, tired face. He came quickly towards her but his footsteps made not a sound in the soft, powdery sand.

'I saw the lights on. Why are you still up, Kelly?' he asked quietly and she heard the concern in his deeply timbred tones as he took her hands into his own. His eyes searched her face. 'You look exhausted. Did something go wrong?'

She shook her head. 'No, nothing.'

'Then why are you still here? It's almost midnight.'

'I was getting myself organised,' she answered simply.

'Until this hour?' He shook his head as though he would never understand her but his gentle smile went straight to her heart and she wondered wistfully why he couldn't always be this nice, so tender and caring. 'Were you waiting up for me?' he added with a curious huskiness as he smoothed her hair back from her face.

Had she? She realised now that she had done exactly that! Had found every excuse in the book to while away the long, lonely hours while she had anxiously awaited his safe return!

'Yes,' she answered truthfully. 'I think I must have been.'

His eyes widened slightly and was it her imagination or did his hand actually tremble as he continued to stroke back her hair?

'That's nice,' he growled. 'Very, very nice.' His warm hand slipped under her chin and he gently tilted it upwards. 'But you shouldn't have, you know,' he scolded. 'You look so tired. You should be in your bed.'

'I know but I . . . I was so worried.'

'Worried?' His surprise was genuine. 'About me?'

'Yes!' Despite the warmth of the tropical evening, she shivered. 'The night is so dark . . . the ocean so deep . . . !'

'Ah, Kelly!' He sighed and pressed his forehead against hers. 'I'd forgotten about your fear of flying.'

'It's just that the plane is so small!' she explained anxiously.

'But it's perfectly safe. I told you that.' He gathered her into his arms, and even though she knew it was only to comfort her, she snuggled gratefully into his strong, reassuring warmth and sighed contentedly.

And then she smelt it!

Smelt the heavy, cloying scent of a very expensive woman's perfume! It clung to the front of his shirt, his collar, the sleeves of his white dinner jacket. It cruelly assaulted her sensitive nostrils and she stiffened and drew quickly away from him, staring up at him with shocked, disbelieving eyes, while feelings of hurt and betrayal swept through her like great and monstrous tidal waves.

Jack tried to draw her once more into his arms, but she stepped rigidly back. His black brows drew together in a puzzled frown. 'What's wrong?'

'N-Nothing.' Her voice sounded hollow. 'I'm just tired! You...you said so yourself.' She added frantically, desperately, as though she might die any moment from sheer exhaustion, 'I *must* go to bed!'

He ran his hand through his wind-tossed hair, sighed deeply and nodded. 'You're absolutely right. I shouldn't be detaining you.' He slipped his arm protectively around her trembling shoulders. 'I'll walk you to your room,' he added softly.

'*No!*' she shrieked. 'I...I can walk there myself.' She shrugged his arm away and started to walk quickly in the direction of the dorm, stumbling in the darkness. There was no moon, no lights and the night was as black as ink. The administration quarters loomed up front, a shadow even deeper than the night. She heard the Jeep door slam and then his long-legged strides catching up to her. Kelly panicked and started to run. A ray of yellow light captured her fleeing figure. Jack grabbed her hand and pressed the torch into it. The light caught the hard, angular lines of his face, the glittering anger in his eyes. His lips parted and the muscles alongside his jaw jerked spasmodically but with a cold determination he checked whatever it was he had been about to say and instead turned abruptly and strode angrily back towards the waiting Jeep.

CHAPTER EIGHT

KELLY heard the Jeep roar off into the inky black night as she raced towards the dormitory, the torch held unsteadily in her flailing hand, the beam bouncing wildly from shadow to shadow. A small, narrow shaft of light coming from one of the rooms served as a beacon and she headed frantically towards it, slipping and sliding in the slippery sand, her breath coming in quick, desperate gasps as though she feared the devil himself was straight on her heels, closing in on her!

She reached the dormitory, ran swiftly along the silent, sleeping veranda towards the door of her room, snatched the key from the pocket of her shorts, let herself in, quickly locked the door behind her and leaned against it, chest heaving as though she had just completed an Olympic marathon. After several minutes, she raised a trembling hand and switched on the overhead light. Her room had never looked so stark, so bare. She walked stiffly over to the window, opened it and turned on the fan. The hot, stuffy air began to move and the small room felt immeasurably cooler. She sank down on the bed and held her head between her hands, desperately trying to analyse her reaction to the perfume she had smelled on Jack's clothing.

Why had it upset her so? Why should she care if he and his colleagues had mixed business with pleasure? And why had it come as such a terrible shock, especially when she *knew* he enjoyed the company of the opposite sex? He had never denied it and certainly wouldn't have placed his luxurious van in such an isolated position if he hadn't planned to have...visitors! And hadn't Max automatically assumed *she* was such a visitor? So *why* had she felt so betrayed? So violated? It didn't make any sense. What her boss did while working or playing was entirely his own affair.

Affair!

Was he having an affair? Had he rushed off for a secret rendezvous with the perfumed lady while only pretending it was a business engagement? Was *she* the reason he had dressed so formally, so handsomely? Kelly moaned softly while her temples throbbed wildly against the palms of her hands. Jack was his own man. He would do what he wanted to do and to hell with anyone else!

'Which includes me!' she sighed aloud as she slowly rose to her feet, grabbed a nightie, a towel, her toiletry bag and headed for the amenities block. Jack's nocturnal excursions were his own concern. Her concerns were her job, the prospect of future jobs and, of course, all that money she was earning. But for once, none of this filled her with its usual joy. All she could feel were the sharp, twisting pains tearing unmercifully at her stomach. Her final lonesome thought for the evening was to hope Jack realised her strange behaviour tonight was simply because she was tired...and not for any other reason.

The heavy pounding on her door awakened her. She sat up in bed, eyes wide, staring in the direction of the door. The pounding continued, followed by a sharp, commanding voice.

'Kelly! Wake up!'

Jack! Why was he knocking on her bedroom door in the middle of the night? Her heart skipped several beats. *Overtime*! she thought wildly. Surely he didn't think that she...that he...that they...!

'Kelly! Open up!'

Kelly jumped out of bed and stood shaking beside it, not knowing what she should do. When the harsh command was repeated, she ran nervously across the floor and whispered hoarsely through the thin wooden structure, 'What do you want?'

'Unlock this door.'

'N-*No*! Go...go away!'

The door shook as he pounded again. Kelly opened the door a wee crack. 'Shh!' she whispered frantically. 'You'll wake up the whole camp.'

'The whole camp *is* awake!'

Her eyes widened. 'Why? What's wrong?'

'That's what I came over to find out!' he thundered. 'Why aren't you over at the mess preparing breakfast?'

She stared at him, convinced she was caught in some ridiculous dream. Here he was at her door, dressed not in pyjamas and a silk black robe as she had somehow imagined, but in work clothes of all things.

'Breakfast?' She laughed shakily. 'In the middle of the night? Are you crazy?'

It was the wrong thing to say, dream or no dream! He pushed the door wide open, stepped inside, kicked it shut with the heel of his work boot. His eyes ripped over her, from the top of her sleep-tousled crown, down the length of her thin cotton nightie to her small, bare feet on the floor.

'So!' he breathed. 'You're not even dressed.' He shook his head in disgust. 'Go back to bed. Max will cover for you.' His voice was stacked in ice and he gave her a final frosty glare before he let himself out of the room and into the thin light of dawn creeping silently across the compound.

Kelly picked up her small travel alarm and stared down at it in disbelieving horror. She had set it for *six* instead of five! Several minutes later, Jack looked up from the worksheet he was discussing with one of his engineers on the veranda of the administration quarters and saw Kelly flying across the compound towards the mess. She was dressed in white shorts, a blue-striped T-shirt and with white sand shoes on her feet. Her rich mane of auburn hair floated behind her like a fire-drenched cloud. He glanced at his wristwatch and smiled. She had made it in eight minutes while he had given her ten!

Breakfast went smoothly and was only a few minutes late due to the preparation of the night before. But Kelly was filled with despair. She had worked hard, doing everything on her own, constantly refusing Max's suggestions that she be provided with a kitchen hand. She had so desperately wanted to prove to Jack that she was a capable, reliable worker, worthy of being given a job in her own profession. Many times she had longed to throw in the towel, thinking she couldn't face another day of standing over a hot stove in an even hotter kitchen, performing the same old chores, peeling and chopping the same old vegetables. Her hands were rough and red from their constant soaking in dishwater, but still she had held on, even planting the little gardens, hoping they might remind him of his promise, that he would at least tell her he hadn't forgotten. All she really wanted was one small word of encouragement, something to tell her there was a light at the end of the tunnel. But no such word had come and she was starting to doubt if it ever would.

Now, added to this despair was another, perhaps even deeper, concern. She had waited up for him, worried about him and had been shaken to the core when she smelled the perfume. She had felt so betrayed! Her cheeks burned with shame at her foolish reaction. Her only consolation was in thinking she wouldn't be seeing him for a while, that he would be working on the site where hopefully he would forget. Then to have him knocking on her door, angry because she wasn't in the kitchen when . . . when she thought he had come to make love to her! Her cheeks burned scarlet as she struggled with her humiliation. She wanted to pack her bags and leave the island before she managed to disgrace herself further.

But she couldn't do that. Not yet. There was her pride to consider. First she had to prove to Jack, once and for all, that not only was she the best darned cook he had ever hired, but also the best employee he had ever known! And once she had proved that . . . and he could no longer do without her . . . and if he hadn't offered her anything on one of his smaller gardening projects . . . *then* she would quit! Leave the high-handed, arrogant, domineering, bully boss in the lurch! Have him beg, *plead*, for her to stay!

But she *wouldn't*!

No, *sirree*!

She pictured herself sitting quietly on a chair in front of his desk, hands folded in her lap, an innocent, 'Well, I *might* reconsider' expression on her face as she listened in round-eyed wonder to his various incentives enticing her to stay.

I'll double your salary! Shorten your hours! How about two assistants? Would you like a dishwasher? An air-conditioner? Breakfast in bed? Just name it, Kelly, and it's yours! What do you say?

Thanks... but no thanks!

She was humming when Jack entered the kitchen shortly before eight. Despite the already-intense heat of the kitchen, she looked cool, fresh, certainly happy, as she placed the last of the clean breakfast dishes back onto their shelves.

'We-e-e-ll!' he drawled, unable to mask his surprise. 'I must say I wasn't expecting such... cheerfulness.'

'Who couldn't help feeling cheerful on such a fine and glorious morning?' She practically sang the words.

'A morning that didn't quite get off to a glorious start,' he gently chided.

'I'm deeply sorry about that.' She managed to look suitably repentant while secretly grateful he hadn't mentioned last night. 'It won't happen again!' She pointed to a huge covered mound on the gleaming counter. 'I've baked the men some fresh blueberry muffins for their morning tea... to make up for the few minutes they had to wait for their breakfasts.'

'Well, I'm sure they will be very pleased,' he answered and wondered what she was up to this time.

Kelly whisked away the clean white tea towel covering the enormous platter piled high with the plump golden muffins. She lightly pressed the backs of her slender fingers against a top one. 'Cool enough to eat.' She picked it up and added invitingly, almost seductively, 'Would you like to try one?'

And suddenly he was reminded of the Garden of Eden and wondered if it was Adam who offered the fatal apple

to Eve or if Eve had offered it to Adam? He rather suspected it was Eve! But what the heck. He took the muffin
and bit into it. It practically melted in his mouth.
'Scrumptious!'

Kelly handed him another and poured him a cup of
coffee. *If this becomes a habit*, she found herself
thinking, *then it will be one of the things he misses most
about me when I leave.* She smiled and refilled his cup.

'Actually, the subject of teas is what I've come to see
you about. We've started work at a new site at the far
end of the island. Time is being needlessly wasted transporting the men back and forth for their scheduled
breaks.'

'I agree. Say no more. Time is money.' She added
briskly, 'I'll pack everything into one of the Jeeps and
take the morning and afternoon teas to the new site until
further notice.'

Jack's brows shot up. *Remarkable!* This was exactly
what he had come to instruct her to do and pretty darn
close to the choice of words he was certain he would
have used.

'I realize it means a lot of extra work for you...' he
began, but Kelly merely shook her head and smiled.

'Not at all. It will actually save work. There will be
no one here to mess up the dining room! Besides,' she
added cheerfully, 'I shall enjoy getting out of the
kitchen.'

Enormously cheered by such cooperation and initiative, especially after her puzzling behaviour the evening
before, Jack sketched her a map of their location and
left her to get on with her chores.

Kelly's smile disappeared as soon as he was gone!
Morning tea delivered to their site? How would she ever

manage the extra work involved and still have lunch ready by twelve? Afternoon tea *also* delivered to their site? How would she ever get dinner on the table for six? She swallowed the panic rising in her throat. This was no time for cold feet. This was above and beyond the call of duty, exactly the sort of opportunity she needed to prove her unquestionable worth. An opportunity made all the sweeter because Jack had provided it himself!

Jack and his engineers would be at the site. She wasn't expected to feed them . . . but she would! Thick slices of ham between equally thick slices of bread, spread with pickles, would undoubtedly be a winner. And so would her muffins served with freshly brewed coffee and the finest of English teas! Cakes, along with an assortment of lush tropical fruits would complete their morning tea. If only she had known earlier she could have fried up some chicken but there was no reason why she couldn't do that tomorrow!

Kelly flew around the kitchen, one eye on the clock, oblivious to the heat, as she prepared the sandwiches, wrapped them up, brewed the coffee, steeped the tea, made up fresh fruit cordial with plenty of ice, poured it all into huge thermal jugs, got the cakes from the freezer, the fruits from the cold room, and finally placed everything onto flat trays along with paper plates, cups, napkins and any utensils she might possibly need.

With morning tea safely out of the way, she quickly set the tables for lunch, popped several large soup bones into a huge cast-iron pot, added a handful of bay leaves, four bunches of chopped celery, a large bag of frozen onions, covered the ingredients with water and placed it on the stove. By the time she had fetched one of the Jeeps, placed the food in the back, washed her face and hands, dragged a brush quickly through her hair, the water in the huge pot had started to boil. She turned the flame down to low, checked to make certain she had the map Jack had drawn for her and set off to make herself totally indispensable.

The Jeep was easy to handle, and now that everything was done and the lunch was simmering happily on the stove, Kelly enjoyed the novelty of transporting the tea to the site. She felt herself relaxing and enjoying the passing scenery of the beautiful, sun-drenched tropical island. The glistening white sand between the vibrant green foliage still reminded her of freshly fallen snow. Kelly knew she was going to miss this place, miss the tranquillity, the exquisite beauty. The Jeep roared up and over small hills. Several times she stopped briefly while on their crests to check on Jack's map, her eyes lingering on his thick, bold scrawls before she would gaze dreamily through the clumps of swaying coconut palms to the sun-sparkled azure blue of the waters breaking gently onto the sugar white shores before she would start on again. The easy clarity of his instructions kept her from becoming hopelessly lost on the dizzying labyrinth of the many tracks and trails leading in and out of the dense tropical foliage.

The increasingly louder sounds of machinery told her she was almost there. She glanced quickly at her watch. Nine-twenty. Only ten minutes to tea break! Kelly pressed down hard on the accelerator. The Jeep spurted eagerly ahead, almost as if it, too, didn't want her to be late, didn't want to jeopardise the start of her plan.

There was barely a clearing where the men were working. Careful preservation of the foliage had been adhered to, and even though the actual construction of

the main buildings was just beginning, it was already
apparent that the natural environment of the island was
going to be an integral part of the entire complex just
as Jack had promised.

Kelly drove slowly into the busy site, seeking out a
shady area in which to park the Jeep and serve the tea.
She quickly found exactly what she was looking for. A
wide grassy area, shaded by a stand of sprawling native
gum trees. Perfect! The men could stretch out on the
soft cushion of grass while enjoying their break. Kelly
parked and started to unload the Jeep, her clear green
eyes darting swiftly over the workers, keenly searching
for one man in particular.

But Jack was not there. Her heart sank while a sharp
spear of disappointment shot through her. *Damn*! Even
though she knew he would undoubtedly hear about the
fabulous morning tea, it wasn't the same as his actually
being here, actually...well, yes, dammit, actually wit-
nessing her triumph.

There was a sudden commotion down at the beach.
Loud shouts of alarm could clearly be heard. The men
cut their machinery, dropped their tools and raced down
a path through the thick green foliage. Kelly was filled
with a deep sense of foreboding, a stomach-crunching
fear. With her heart in her mouth, she, too, abandoned
her chores and raced swiftly down to the beach.

A temporary steel jetty, similar but much wider and
longer than the one used to offload supplies at the camp,
stretched from the shore out to sea. Aligned beside it
and banking dangerously was a shallow draft barge. A
huge yellow crane was stationed on the jetty, unloading
a bulky piece of machinery from the heaving barge. Word
quickly spread that a cable had slipped and snapped on

the crane, rendering the frantic crane operator incapable of controlling the heavy steel coil or from preventing the cargo from swinging haphazardly in the air. Jack stood on the jetty, shouting instructions up to the operator, gesturing with his hands. The vagrant cable quickly picked up speed as it arched freely, causing the attached machine to spin crazily on its end as if it was little more than a child's harmless toy.

The men on the beach grew silent. Everyone was ordered to stand well back. The machine could break loose and catapult onto the beach at any moment. There was the unmistakable stench of fear. Kelly stood with the men, eyes rounded in horror, heart thumping wildly in her chest. Jack jumped onto the base of the crane and was slowly climbing the narrow tower! The machine swung around him, each time narrowly missing his head. She wanted to scream and must have, for one of the men, a supervisor living in one of the temporary houses near the dorm, put his arm quickly, firmly, around her shoulders.

'Quiet!' he sharply commanded her. 'For God's sake, don't distract him! Everyone! Get farther back. That machine is getting ready to fly!'

The desperate urgency in his voice only intensified Kelly's fear, her horror of what was happening. Jack climbed steadily higher, and higher still, the chain swinging madly now, the heavy machine arching closer and closer to his body, finally brushing close enough for the resultant breeze to whip the protective hard hat from his head. There was an immediate collective gasp from the men and the supervisor quickly clamped his hand over Kelly's mouth, smothering her terrified scream as she watched the hat tumbling down, down, in dreadful slow-motion horror, to finally drop into the foaming sea.

Miraculously, Jack reached the top of the crane. They could hear him roaring orders to the operator below. There was a harsh meshing of gears as the driver frantically attempted to obey his instructions. Jack slowly, stealthily, inched his way on his stomach across the narrow, swinging beam to the offending cable, occasionally shouting commands or making quick, sharp gestures with his hands as to what he wanted done. The bulky machine continued to swing dizzily, dangerously around him.

From a tool belt attached to his waist, Jack removed a huge spanner, shouted several more orders in quick succession to the now remarkably calm operator, and together they brought the arm of the crane under control. The swinging slowly ceased and then stopped altogether. The machine was gently, slowly, carefully lowered and finally released safely onto the jetty. Jack inched his way back along the beam, slid agilely down the steep, narrow tower and finally, thankfully, stepped onto the safety of the steel platform.

A resounding cheer and a burst of applause erupted from the men. Hats were tossed into the air. Several raced into the still-foaming surf to retrieve Jack's safety helmet. The supervisor released Kelly and she sank slowly to her knees in the sand, her throat sore, parched, as though she had been screaming the whole of the time.

Oblivious to the sensation he had caused, Jack stood calmly wiping his hands on an oily rag while talking to the crane operator and the engineers who had quickly joined them. Together they began an immediate examination of the crane and the offending coil. The men on the beach started trekking back to the site, talking cheerfully, shouting and joking amongst themselves. A few called out to Kelly, enquiring about their mid-morning tea. She rose slowly to her feet, shaken, dazed, heart still pumping wildly, unable to comprehend that everything could so easily return to normal, that no one was apparently giving a second thought to the very real possibility that Jack could have been killed or badly injured. They were treating it as if it was part of the job, all in a day's work.

With a violently trembling hand, Kelly brushed the sand from her quivering knees, her eyes fastened to the man who had risked his life to save a machine. *Stupid! Bloody stupid!* Jack looked up, frowned at the sight of her rigid form, at the eyes far too dark set in a face far too white. He turned abruptly to the supervisor who had held her, said something, the supervisor nodded, shrugged. Jack's frown deepened and his mouth hardened as he made his way quickly along the jetty and across the beach to where she stood.

Kelly watched him walk towards her as though they were both taking part in some incredible Spielberg movie. Nothing seemed real anymore. His blue denim shirt had been ripped from the belted waist of his black work shorts and several buttons were missing. His face and hands were smudged with grease and his hair was mussed, wind-blown and slightly tangled. He had never looked more attractive, more...*dear*! And when he came closer, to stand right in front of her, she wanted desperately to take him in her arms, cradle his head, stroke his hard cheeks, touch him, reassure herself that he was all right.

'You shouldn't have come down here, Kelly,' he said sternly, but his hand was surprisingly gentle as he reached out to touch the chalky whiteness of her cheek.

'I wanted to watch the show!' she quivered.

His eyes narrowed slightly as they skimmed over her pale face. 'The show is over,' he stated quietly.

'What?' Her voice rose, became shrill, accusing, verging on hysteria. 'It's *over*? The high wire act is *over*? There's to be no *encores*? No *grand finales*? No... *nothing*?'

Anger flared briefly in his eyes. 'None.' He dragged a weary hand roughly through his tangled hair. 'Don't make a scene, Kelly. Go up and serve tea.'

'You're so good at giving orders!' she hissed. 'Why didn't you order one of your men to climb that crane?' Her voice broke. 'Why did it have to be *you*?'

'Because I'm the boss! I would never consider placing any of my people in a potentially dangerous situation!'

'And what if something had happened to you?' Tears sparkled in her eyes. 'What if you had been k-killed? What would become of your people then? Who... who would keep them in a job? Who would p-pay them?'

His head jerked back as though she had struck him. 'So!' he breathed. 'That's what this is all about?' His laugh was cold, bitter. 'I should have known. The concern... the tears... they're not for me. They're for yourself!' He laughed again but as before there was no humour in the sound. 'Don't worry, Kelly, I intend to be around for a long time yet. You'll receive your pay.' His eyes ground coldly into hers. 'Now get the hell up there and earn it!'

With a strangled sob, Kelly turned and fled up the path. With every step she took, she wanted only to turn

back and tell him how thankful she was that he was safe,
how terrified she had been that he might have been hurt.
But how could she after what she had just said to him?
Another sob tore from her throat. How could he have
believed it? How could he possibly believe the torture
she had just endured had been prompted by a callous
concern for her pay? Did he really think she could be
so heartless, so uncaring, so unfeeling, so *mercenary*?

Kelly stood shivering from reaction at the edge of the
path, hidden by a fringe of trees. It took several deep,
steadying breaths before she felt capable of stepping into
the clearing and making her way stiffly towards the Jeep,
only to find the food had already been despatched and
the men sitting around in groups, enjoying it.

Which left her nothing to do except hide her despair
and wait for them to finish so she could pack up and
return to camp. She kept her eyes on the path, desperately hoping Jack would appear at any minute. She knew
he wouldn't talk to her. All she wanted was to see him
again, to reassure herself that he was indeed all right.
The minutes dragged by with an agonizing slowness until
finally she had to admit that he wasn't coming, that he
and his engineers had stayed behind to continue work
on the crane. She carefully packed their sandwiches into
an Esky with a bag of ice to keep them fresh, added
some fruit, snapped the lids shut, picked up a Thermos
of coffee and instructed a young apprentice to take it
down to the men still at the beach. 'Make sure you tell
them I want that Esky and Thermos back!'

When Kelly returned to camp, she immediately checked
on the simmering soup, added extra spices, several more
vegetables, some pasta, two gallon tins of tomatoes,
spread eighty thick slices of bread with grated cheese

and chives to toast later in the oven, made up a variety of fruit juices, decided on strawberry custard served over chocolate sponge cakes for dessert, set the tables and finally unloaded the Jeep.

And while she silently toiled in the blistering heat, tortured by her incredibly insensitive words and haunted by the terrifying images of Jack high up on the crane, with that monstrous machine flying closer and closer to his unprotected body, Kelly realised she couldn't go ahead with her plan. It would be easy enough for him to replace her, especially considering the salary and this beautiful tropical island, but still, realistically, it couldn't happen overnight. No, she wouldn't leave him in the lurch as she had originally planned. That wouldn't be fair. She decided to work a month longer before giving him a week's notice, maybe even two weeks'. A month would be all she really needed to truly prove her worth. And then . . . she swallowed hard . . . and then she would be on her way . . . but she would have done it with dignity.

At twelve noon the men arrived at the mess for lunch. They talked incessantly about Jack and his heroics while inadvertently forcing Kelly to relive the nightmare. She was relieved when the trucks finally arrived to transport them back to the construction site. Several minutes later, Jack walked in carrying the Thermos and Esky. Kelly was at the sink, elbow-deep in dishwater. 'Where do you want these?' he asked brusquely.

Kelly didn't look up from her work. She was trying desperately to ignore the wild thrashings of her heart. 'Just over there will be fine,' she answered stiffly.

'Over where?' he asked irritably.

Tears rushed to her eyes at his tone. 'On the counter by. . . by the stove,' she answered in a muffled voice.

She heard him walk over to the counter and place the items down before joining her at the sink. He picked up a glass, turned on the tap and poured himself some water. She felt his eyes burning into her as he raised the glass to his mouth, swallowed, filled it again, rinsed it out and placed it back down. Then he was gone. He had been in the kitchen for barely more than a minute or two but Kelly felt totally drained. She leaned weakly against the sink and placed a trembling hand to her chest. Her heart felt as if it had been dragged, kicking and screaming, through a raging tornado!

Max sauntered over later while Kelly was loading up the Jeep with provisions for the men's afternoon tea. 'They never stop eating, do they?' Max chuckled as she helpfully picked up one of the Eskies and shoved it into the back of the vehicle.

'It certainly seems that way,' Kelly sighed listlessly and loaded another.

'I hear there was a bit of excitement down at the jetty,' Max stated casually.

Kelly hesitated. 'A . . . a bit.'

'You handle it okay?'

Kelly cleared her throat. 'Did you hear otherwise?'

'Sure did!' Max chuckled. 'Heard you were screaming and carrying on something wicked!'

Kelly's face turned a bright pink. 'Is that what...what Jack told you?'

'No, Eddie. Said he had to clamp your mouth to keep you quiet!' She wrapped a sympathetic arm around Kelly's small shoulders. 'You mustn't let it get to you, kid,' she clucked. 'Those sorts of things happen all the time on construction sites. But the Boss knows what he's doing. He's climbed many a rig, many a times, and some much higher than that crane. It's a scary business all right, but you'll get used to it.' She patted Kelly reassuringly on the back. 'You'll see.'

Kelly smiled weakly. 'I suppose you're right.'

But she had no intention of getting used to it nor did she believe she ever could. With Max's help, the last of the trays were loaded onto the Jeep and Kelly climbed behind the wheel.

'Max,' she began slowly, 'how easy is it to find a cook, good or otherwise, to work in a construction camp?'

'Not easy at all. In fact, it's darned near impossible.'

Kelly's fine brows shot up in surprise. 'Impossible?' she echoed. 'Really?'

'Uh-huh.' Max leaned against the side of the Jeep, hands thrust into the pockets of her jeans. 'Even when this becomes a luxury resort,' she continued as she glanced around at the rather primitive camp, 'it will still be mighty hard to find good staff, harder still to keep them.'

'Really?' Kelly said again, frowning deeply. This wasn't at all what she had expected to hear. 'I...I wouldn't have thought so.'

'Oh, yes,' Max sighed. 'The allure of a tropical island, magical though it may be, quickly fades after a few months. It's the isolation,' she confided knowingly. 'It gets to people after a while.'

Kelly sat rigidly in her seat. 'So the Boss must have been very pleased...when I accepted this position?'

'Well, I know *I* was when he told me.'

'But what about Jack?' Kelly persisted. 'Was he pleased, too?'

'He was relieved more than anything.'

'How relieved?' Kelly urged.

'Greatly relieved. We had a cook lined up, and only after much negotiating I can assure you, when he went and did the dirty on us and pulled out at the very last minute. Said he had a crook back!' Max added in disgust.

'So the Boss must have been out of his mind with worry,' Kelly mused softy in a strained, distant-sounding voice, as though speaking only to herself. 'And desperately seeking another cook?'

No wonder he had offered her the job and sweetened it with a salary he knew she couldn't refuse and a promise he had no intention of ever fulfilling. It wasn't to help her out as she had so naïvely thought. And it certainly wasn't because he had felt badly or even a little bit guilty over what he had done to her. No, he had simply used her, taken advantage of her desperate situation. He had used her to solve his own problems!

Bile rose bitterly at the back of her throat when she remembered how worried she had been that she mightn't be up to the job, how quickly she had jumped to carry out his commands, how she had slaved in the blistering heat of the kitchen all day, every day, from dawn to dusk, never complaining about the conditions, hoping only to please him, hoping for a small word of praise, while all along he had been enormously grateful to have any cook at all.

And she thought of how she had waited up for him, worried about him, and how upset she had been over the perfume. She thought of the paralysing fear she had suffered when he had been up on the crane. And how she had decided to alter her plan to save him any inconvenience. She almost choked!

Well, there would be no dignity! She would return to her original plan. Leave him in the lurch! Then noticing the strange look Max was giving her, Kelly managed to gather herself together. 'Yes, he must have been very pleased with himself when I accepted the job. After all, a camp must have a cook!'

'Can't do without 'em!' Max promptly agreed, and wondered at the fierce, unnatural brightness burning in Kelly's eyes while her usually rosy complexion was noticeably pale, except for the two hot spots of feverish colour high on her cheekbones.

'Anyway,' Max added with an uneasy chuckle, 'why so many questions? Thinking about hitting the Boss for a raise in pay?'

Kelly's head shot up. She glared at Max, green eyes blazing. 'Why would you ask such a thing?'

Max's eyes widened in surprise, totally taken aback by Kelly's strong reaction. 'Dearie me, I was only joking.'

'Well, I don't think it was funny!' Kelly's hands shook as she turned the key in the ignition. The Jeep shot off in a cloud of white, swirling dust leaving a very bemused Max in its wake.

CHAPTER NINE

THE grumblings from the young apprentices and labourers had started innocently enough but lately it had become much worse. At first it was merely small demands for extra helpings—extra potatoes, extra dessert, more coffee—but Kelly soon realised extras weren't the issue here. They were simply excuses to remain longer in the dining room in the evenings, to postpone even for a few minutes the inevitable return to the loneliness of their rooms.

And while they were always freshly showered and in clean clothes for their evening meal and didn't venture into the dining room before Kelly banged her gong, eventually all managed to hang around the mess after dinner until nine o'clock when supper was served. They spent their time in between bickering and arguing amongst themselves. In desperation and hoping to occupy them, Kelly asked for volunteers to sweep the floor, clear the tables, dry the dishes, but those who did were so teased by the others that eventually they stopped and rejoined the fray.

It was easy to see a storm was brewing. They had become used to the demands and rigours of their jobs, and now that they had, boredom and restlessness had settled in. The youngsters, as Kelly sometimes affectionately referred to them, were obviously missing families and friends. She felt sorry for them and decided to do something about their plight before handing in her resignation. She couldn't leave knowing they were unhappy after having looked after them for so long.

'I need to speak to Jack,' Kelly told Max when she managed to squeeze time from her hectic schedule to dash across to the administration quarters. 'Can you set up a ... an appointment?'

'Are you sure it's important?'

'I wouldn't be here unless it was, Max.'

'I realise that but you know how busy the Boss is, how strapped for time. Right now he's in Brisbane holding meetings with his architects, so unless it's an absolute emergency ... a crisis ... anything that I can't help you with, then really, in all fairness to the man, I can't ...'

'I have no intention of wasting his time,' Kelly answered stiffly, 'nor yours, nor mine! I realise he can't see me now. I heard him fly out early this morning, but what about when he gets back tonight?'

'That won't be until late.'

'How late?'

'Midnight or so.'

'Can you contact him?'

'Of course.'

'Then would you please tell him I'll meet him at the airstrip. Tell him it's not an emergency but that it *is* important. We can talk about it while driving back to camp. That way nobody's time will be wasted.'

'We-e-e-ll,' Max sighed, realising by the determined look on Kelly's face that there would be no point in arguing. 'I'll put it to him and see what he says. But don't be too disappointed if he doesn't agree,' she added warningly. 'He'll have a lot on his mind when he gets back, and knowing him, will be up half, if not most of the night, working on changes he's proposed to his architects.' Max shook her head. 'The man's been driving himself like there's no tomorrow,' she muttered, obviously worried, 'but either way, I'll let you know,' she promised.

Later in the day, Max informed Kelly that as it wasn't an emergency, the Boss hadn't agreed to her meeting him at the airstrip but said he would certainly try to find some time for her during the next few days.

Try? Kelly inwardly fumed. Jack had been deliberately avoiding her these past few weeks, speaking to her only when necessary, his tone always polite, courteous, but cold, reserved. Well, he wasn't going to avoid her this time. Boredom and discontent amongst the workers could be dangerous on a building site. Deliberately ignoring the message, Kelly picked up a spare Jeep at eleven forty-five that evening and drove out to the airstrip.

Stars twinkled and flickered like a mass of priceless diamonds sprinkled across a blanket of luxurious black velvet in the soft tropical sky. Crickets from the surrounding bush chirped in perfect harmony and added to Kelly's strange feeling of nervous excitement. Meeting Jack at the airstrip seemed such a romantically intimate thing to be doing...especially at such a bewitching hour! Especially when he had told her not to!

A large kangaroo suddenly hopped onto the middle of the narrow dirt track straight in front of the small Jeep. Kelly quickly brought the vehicle to a skidding halt. The beast blinked lazily into the twin beams of the headlights before sauntering off to the other side.

'Thanks, sport!' Kelly shifted gears and shot past him before he decided to spring out again.

She parked the Jeep beside the one Jack had driven out earlier that morning and glanced nervously at her watch. It was close to midnight. The sky was so crowded with stars that at first she didn't see the one that was actually moving, coming closer, floating steadily downwards. Her heart seemed to catch its breath before it started to beat again. *Jack!*

The small aircraft dropped lower in the sky. Kelly squeezed her eyes shut and didn't open them again until she heard the *Jabiru* land safely and come to a complete halt. The door opened and for a moment her heart stood quite still as his huge frame filled the narrow space. A black leather briefcase was tucked under one arm, his tie was loosened around the strong brown column of his neck and a lightweight tweed jacket was slung casually over one broad shoulder. He took a deep breath of the sweetly scented tropical air before jumping down from the plane, the light breeze catching his coal black hair and sweeping it away from his brow.

Kelly stepped out of the Jeep without realising she had even moved and stood transfixed beside it. Her own hair was a shimmering mass of russet silk framing the perfect oval of her face and brushing against the smoothness of her bare shoulders. The breeze tugged at the skirt of her white sleeveless sun frock with its tiny shoestring straps and flicked it teasingly around her slender calves. But she wasn't aware of any of this. Her *world* stood in front of her, strong, tall and silent in front of the plane. She felt herself floating towards him, quite as if some invisible threads were drawing her to his side.

She forgot about her mission, why she was there. She wanted only to take this tired, handsome giant of a man safely home to his van, make him a cup of coffee, a sandwich, listen to the events of his day, gently massage his temples, his shoulders, run her fingers caressingly through his thick, wiry hair, wrap her arms lovingly around his neck, press her lips to his...

He saw her then. Saw the pale, almost ghostly vision of loveliness floating towards him. But Kelly didn't see the sudden tightening of his mouth, the quickening of his shoulder muscles, the flash of anger sear his eyes. Nor did she hear the woman's voice behind him! Therefore she was totally unprepared for the dreadful paralysing shock she felt when he turned abruptly to help someone down from the plane, someone blonde and beautiful, someone whose gay laughter floated across the scented air as the billowing skirts of her rose-coloured evening gown flounced high above her thighs.

Kelly stopped, stunned. The world seemed to spin in front of her before the ground rose and smacked her in the face. Her heart rocked violently in her chest, smashing against her ribcage before rocketing down to her stomach. Nausea rose to her throat and she raised a small, trembling hand to her mouth. The breeze captured her tiny, agonised moan and tossed it recklessly to the wind.

Jack's eyes, still angry, never left Kelly's pale, hauntingly beautiful face as he and his companion walked towards her. The blonde seemed fascinated by the silent white figure standing so still on the sandy strip who had obviously come to meet them but apparently not to greet them. She murmured something to Jack, but he didn't reply. They came closer...and it was only then that Kelly smelled the *perfume*. Every nerve, every sense in her body recoiled against it while her poor battered heart screamed in silent agony.

And with her suffering finally came the shocking truth. *She loved him*! *Oh, God, how she loved him*! And she realised she had fallen in love with him probably the very first moment she had laid eyes on him. He had hurt her, humiliated her, taken everything she had but she had never once suspected he had also stolen her heart!

Now she knew why she had gone to him for help, cast aside her pride, begged for a job. It was because she knew he would be leaving for Brisbane and she was terrified she might never see him again. Now she knew why she had accepted the position as cook and it hadn't been for the money or even for the promise as she had so foolishly convinced herself. She would have worked for nothing, done anything...just to be near him. Even the weeks living in the shack at Bargara had been only so she might see him, catch small glimpses of him whenever he came to inspect his town houses.

No wonder she had been so terrified when he had been up on that crane. The possibility of her love being hurt was more than she could bear. No wonder he had only to look at her and she would melt into his arms! No wonder he could so easily hurt her! And...and no wonder she had wanted to make herself totally indispensable! Tears formed a painful lump at the back of her throat. *It was simply a pathetic guise by a lovestruck fool trying desperately to trick the man she loved into believing that he couldn't let her go, that he loved her, too*!

'Kelly, this is Amanda Geering, one of our top architects.' Jack's brusque voice broke into her silent, painful reverie. 'Kelly is our cook,' he added to the blonde, and before either woman could murmur acknowledgement, Jack firmly steered Amanda over to the Jeep he had driven to the airstrip that morning and helped her inside. He tossed his jacket, briefcase and Amanda's small, Paisley-embroidered suitcase into the back before returning to Kelly. Kelly watched the whole operation without blinking, watched him move closer, watched the anger glitter in his eyes.

'I find it impossible to believe Max forgot to give you my message,' he growled disapprovingly and, taking her arm, led her over to the other Jeep.

'She . . . she didn't forget.'

He nodded, his expression grim. 'That's what I thought! You simply decided to ignore her instructions.'

'Not hers.' She swallowed hard. '*Yours*!'

'I see!' His dark blue eyes sparkled dangerously. 'Well, in that case, this had better be good! And quick!' He opened the door, helped her inside and slid in beside her. 'All right, Kelly,' he sighed. 'Talk to me. What's the problem?'

Kelly felt she was suffocating. He was so close to her, facing her, his eyes holding hers, his arm stretched out on the back of her seat brushing against her hair, his hard, muscular thigh pressed against the quivering softness of her own. She could smell the tantalising aroma of his aftershave, the clean, intoxicating male scent of his body. Her hands trembled in her lap and she quickly lowered her head, terrified he might guess, terrified he might see what was in her eyes, what he had done to her heart. The silence was oppressive but she didn't dare risk speaking or looking up at him.

'Well?' he growled impatiently and made a point of looking at his watch. 'I haven't got all night, Kelly. What's so important that it obviously couldn't wait?'

'I . . . I can't talk now,' she whispered hoarsely.

'Can't talk now?' he exploded. 'Obviously you couldn't wait to talk... and now you have the nerve to say you *can't*?' He shook his head, clearly vexed.

'I... I'm sorry, it's just that I... I'm not feeling well,' she whispered and struggled to keep from dying.

'Not feeling well?' He placed a cool, firm hand on her brow. The gesture was so caring, so gentle, that Kelly thought her heart would split in two. He opened the door, got out and took her hand. 'You will drive back with us. I'll send someone for the Jeep in the morning.'

'*No!*' Her strangled voice was filled with alarm as she pulled her hand free and shrank back in her seat.

He stood looking down at her, black brows drawn together in a puzzled frown. 'What's wrong now?'

'I... I want to drive back by myself!'

'You're too sick to talk but not too sick to drive? Even for you, that doesn't make a great deal of sense! Come on, now,' he added gently and reached for her hand again but she whimpered like a frightened, wounded animal and shrank even farther back in her seat, her eyes two dark, tortured holes in the paleness of her face. Jack frowned his concern. 'What is it? What's wrong?'

'Nothing!' she answered quickly, far too quickly.

He leaned towards her, placed his hand under her chin and forced her to look up at him, his own eyes dark, intent, searching. 'Don't push me, Kelly,' he stated softly. 'You know I don't take kindly to provocation.'

Her control snapped. She wanted to lash out at him, hurt him, run her fingernails down his handsome cheeks, poke his eyes out, grab his heart and stomp on it the way he had stomped on her own. 'And I don't take kindly to being told to wait every time I need to speak with you!' she shouted.

The Jeep shot forwards narrowly missing his feet. Jack stared in utter disbelief as the careering vehicle rocketed wildly down the track. Cursing loudly, he jumped behind the wheel of the other Jeep and made pursuit while the startled Amanda wisely held on!

The beams following her formed a blinding blur of brilliant light in Kelly's rear-view mirror. Tears streamed down her cheeks as she recklessly picked up speed, silently praying that no unsuspecting wildlife would dart across her path. A sharp corner loomed ahead and she took it far too fast, spinning out of control, riding high on two wheels, almost rolling the Jeep before the small vehicle miraculously straightened itself and leapt forward again, picking up even more speed as it continued its perilous journey. The trailing beam of lights immediately distanced themselves and she knew Jack had stopped his pursuit.

But still she didn't slow down, speeding straight into camp and coming to a shuddering halt in front of the dormitory. She raced into her room and locked the door behind her, leaning against it until she heard Jack roar past, then she collapsed into a tangled, broken heap on her bed, torturing herself with images of Jack and Amanda making love on his enormous king-size bed with the bright royal blue satin spread.

Kelly didn't know how long she lay there—minutes, days, years, or even if she had slept—before she heard a key turn in the lock. She struggled unsuccessfully to raise herself. The door opened. Jack stood there, rigid, stiff, filled with his anger. Without taking his eyes from her tear-stained face, he stepped quietly into the room and locked the door.

Kelly half scrambled, half fell from the bed and, with her heart thumping madly in her chest, stared up at him. He looked wild! His eyes were ablaze with fury, an angry flush mopped his hard cheeks and his thick mane of black hair was hopelessly mussed from the wind. With a cruel smile, he jerked the tie from his neck, allowed it to dangle from his hand, strode over to the opened window, banged it shut. The anger in his eyes mounted as she stood in front of him.

'Get undressed!' he ordered in a soft voice.

'What?' she gasped and stepped shakily backwards.

'You heard me!' He circled her neck with the tie and pulled her towards him. 'I'm going to do what I should have done right from the very beginning!' The tie fell soundlessly to the floor as he slipped his dark hands beneath the tiny straps of her white dress and eased them off the silky smoothness of her bare shoulders before unzipping the back. The dress fluttered around her slender body as it drifted lazily to the floor, leaving her entirely naked except for a pair of silk white panties.

'Don't do this!' Kelly pleaded and crossed her arms over her breasts.

'Don't do *what*? *This*?' He pinned her wrists behind her back with one huge hand and cupped a small breast with the other.

'Or *this*?' He dipped his dark, unruly head and kissed her hard on the mouth before burning a blazing trail of kisses down the slender column of her throat.

'Or is it *this* you don't want me to do?' He picked her up and dropped her onto the bed, his eyes holding her trapped as he stood above her, slowly undoing the buttons of his shirt. He eased it off his massive shoulders, the muscles rippling under the tanned smoothness of his skin. He tossed the shirt carelessly onto the desk before his hands moved down to the buckle on his belt.

Kelly's heart leapt all over her chest as she followed his movements. She simply couldn't take her eyes off him nor did she want to. There wasn't an ounce of excess flesh on his hard, lean, muscular body. He was perfect, magnificent! He was absolutely beautiful! Her fingers trembled and her heart became tightly wedged in her throat as she struggled with her overwhelming desire to reach up and stroke his smooth, tanned skin, run them lightly over the contours of his muscles and feel the silky black hairs sprinkled across his massive chest. She forgot all the hurts, the humiliations, the promise he had no intention of keeping. She forgot Amanda! In desperation, she squeezed her eyes tightly shut but he had already seen her desire, and it was every bit as naked and as bold as his own. He laughed softly and joined her on the bed to begin the seduction that would make her his slave!

Jack was a man who didn't believe in short cuts, a man who gave everything he had, left no stone unturned, a man who sincerely believed any job worth doing was worth doing well. He made love to every part of her body, making her cry out in ecstasy and beg for more. He made her his! And when it was all over, and he raised himself on his elbows and smiled down at her, Kelly's eyes were soft, beautiful, dusky with passion. Her cheeks were rosy and small tendrils of hair clung damply to her temples. Her lips were a bright red, swollen from the passion of his kisses.

'Are you OK?' he murmured gruffly and gently stroked back the clinging tendrils from her hot cheeks.

'Yes,' she whispered and there was certainly no pain in her lovestruck eyes. She reached up and lovingly stroked his hard cheeks then ran her fingertips lightly across his lips. 'Now it's your turn,' she added huskily. 'Roll onto your back!'

And Jack discovered to his enormous delight that Kelly shared in his philosophy, that nothing should be done in halves, that no stone should ever be left unturned, that any job worth doing was certainly worth doing well. And when all these philosophies had been well and truly dealt with, and they lay exhausted in each other's arms, Jack finally managed to raise himself from the bed, grab his shirt, pull Kelly to her feet, drape it around her dainty shoulders, reach for a towel she had left hanging over a chair and tie it snugly around his waist. 'We'll go for a swim,' he announced and added with a grin so wonderfully boyish that it did quite marvellous things to her already buoyant heart, 'To cool ourselves down!' He took her hand and led her across the room.

'But what if someone sees us?' Kelly whispered nervously as he opened the door.

'Everyone's asleep but just in case someone does they will see we're simply going for a swim on a very hot, very still night.' He squeezed her hand. 'There's no harm in that, is there?'

She looked into his cycs and hcr hcart somersaulted. 'No harm at all!' she agreed.

Kelly couldn't believe this was happening to her. Couldn't believe the man she so desperately loved had actually walked straight into her room, claimed her, made love to her in a way she had never dreamed possible, had totally possessed her, made her his own. And now here she was, wearing nothing but his shirt, he nothing but her towel, with only the twinkling stars to guide them, hand in hand, like the lovers they were, to have a swim in the ocean while the whole camp slept. It was so special, so wonderfully romantic. She thought her heart would surely burst with the sheer blissful joy of her happiness.

The white sand seemed even brighter at night lit as it was by the magic of the stars. But then she saw that the moon had come out and it seemed such a gloriously thoughtful thing for the moon to have done, to shine down on her and her love. Jack removed the towel from around his waist and spread it across the warm sand. He stood there, tall, tanned, gloriously naked under the moonlight, like a proud warrior, a Greek god.

How she loved him! She desperately wanted to tell him so, express her wondrous feelings, and she was so filled with these emotions, so consumed with the love she felt for this man that mere words seemed not enough, seemed hopelessly inadequate for what she was feeling. If only... if only she could reach up and pluck the twinkling stars from the heavens above she could place them on the sand before his feet and spell out her love. And then ... and then he would know, know how deeply she loved him.

'Come on, Kelly,' he urged, his deep velvet voice seeming to float magically in the scented tropical breeze, the few simple words mingling with the sounds of the rustling palms fringing the beach as he reached out to remove her shirt.

Kelly stepped suddenly back, her hair falling across her soft cheeks as she lowered her head, clutching the folds of the shirt in front of her, completely overcome by her feelings, choked with her urgency to tell him about them.

'Don't be shy,' he chided gently as he drew her nearer to him. 'We have no secrets from each other.'

No secrets? Her love for him was a secret. Her plan was a secret. She peeped up at him, desperately yearning to tell him everything, tell him how she was feeling, to share with him the overwhelming joy of her heart. But something...something was holding her back. What was it? What she she so *afraid* of?

His hands slipped possessively under the shirt, hard and firm against her bare skin. Kelly immediately stiffened and held her breath, deliberately trying to prevent her body from responding. But it was too late. The fires had been ignited, were already burning out of control. She loved him; she wanted him; there was nothing she could do about it...nor did she wish to.

The shirt slid slowly down her body and fell in a crumpled heap by her bare feet. Kelly impatiently kicked it aside and stepped even closer to him, wrapped her slender arms lovingly, tightly, possessively, around his neck. She felt the great thumping of his heart against her hot cheek and she unwrapped her arms and slid her hands caressingly down his back to trail over the smoothness of his muscles.

'Kelly!' he groaned and crushed her against him, his mouth hot and urgent on her own. There was a tingling in the pit of her stomach and her knees weakened and then he was gently easing her down into the soft bed of sand, kissing her, whispering his desire for each part of her body. The waves crashed around them, the stars and the moon shone above them, and these were the only witnesses to their love.

Later, when they stood at the water's edge, silently facing but not touching each other, naked bodies glistening, the soft foam swirling gently around their feet, Jack took in a great heaving breath and expelled it in a long, ragged sigh. He tilted his head back and glanced up at the flickering stars without really seeing them. He lowered his head again almost immediately to gaze at Kelly between black, spiky lashes. Her beautiful slender body glowed like pale marble under the soft moonlight. He wanted her again. He couldn't seem to get enough of her.

He took another deep, steadying breath and once more forced himself to look away from her, to look out at the sea, but it was to no avail. He could feel her watching him. Could actually *feel* those great big beautiful green eyes burning into his skin... and he had to look back at her.

Their eyes held each other captive for several nerve-tingling seconds before Kelly turned suddenly and fled into the sea, her glorious russet mane flowing freely, provocatively, behind her. The hard line of his mouth relaxed into a smile as he watched her splash playfully in the surf and shallow dive between the waves. But each time she dove, her smooth, perfect body, wet and glistening under the moonlight, peeked invitingly up at him through the star-studded surf.

'Come on, Kelly, that's enough. Out you get.'

Her eyes widened in surprise. 'Out? But aren't you coming in?'

'No!'

'No? But it was your idea we come for a swim,' she reminded him and he watched her shallow dive again in the waist-deep surf.

'Yes, well... it's getting late.'

'But it will only take a minute for a quick dip,' she told him and, holding her small nose, ducked her head backwards into the surf and emerged with her hair flattened against her head. Her teeth sparkled whitely as she grinned at him and never had she looked or seemed more beautiful. 'Or can't you swim?' she added playfully. 'Or are you just chicken?' she continued to tease.

His warning glance, even though it contained a slight element of amusement, was enough to convince her that her schoolgirlish taunts hadn't affected him. Not that she had believed for an instant that they would, of course. She was merely stalling for time, wanting to prolong the most magical evening of her entire life, wishing it could go on forever. He picked up the towel, tied it firmly about his waist, retrieved the shirt and held it out in front of him, obviously expecting her to leave the surf and step obediently into it.

Kelly flipped onto her back, floating contentedly, deliberately pretending she hadn't seen him pick up the towel, tie it around his waist, or hold the shirt out for her. 'The water's great. Really warm. I could stay here forever!'

'I'm losing my patience, Kelly,' he stated and his voice was a deep rumbling growl reaching her from across the gentle swell of the waves.

Kelly flipped onto her stomach and smiled at him. 'Come and get me!' she purred provocatively.

There was a heavy silence before he spoke. 'You'll be sorry if I do!'

'How sorry?' she teased and her voice tinkled like tiny bells across the waves.

The towel and shirt were discarded as he dove into the surf. Kelly shrieked her delight as his powerful arms ate up the short distance separating them. She waited until he had almost reached her before she executed a neat dive into an oncoming wave. Suddenly she felt herself being lifted high out of the water and looking down into a pair of dark, incredibly blue eyes.

For a moment he simply held her there, suspended in the air, the water cascading down her slender body, forming small rivulets between her breasts, over her tummy and against her thighs. He lowered her but instead of holding her against him as she fully expected he would, as she wanted him to do, he tossed her over his shoulder, ignored her kicks and screams, ploughed back to the beach and dumped her unceremoniously onto the soft, powdery white sand.

'Is that sorry enough?' he demanded triumphantly, obviously pleased with his efforts as she lay sprawled by his feet.

'Spoilsport!' Kelly muttered.

Jack chuckled and helped her up from her ungracious position. He retrieved the shirt and draped it once more around her slender shoulders before kissing the tip of her nose and then her mouth and finally turning her in the direction of the path leading up to camp. 'Go straight to bed,' he ordered.

Kelly turned back to him confusion clouding her eyes. 'Aren't you coming with me?'

'No, I'm going for a swim.'

A deep stabbing hurt filled her as she watched him run down to the surf and dive neatly into an oncoming wave. After several painful moments, she clutched his shirt more tightly around herself and walked slowly back to the dorm. Once inside her room, Kelly quickly bundled his clothes into the shirt, tied it by the arms, slipped into her dressing gown and went outside to lean casually against the veranda rail, determined not to show him how deeply he had wounded her feelings. After several minutes, she began to feel uneasy and her eyes anxiously searched the long, drifting shadows.

No one should ever swim alone, she silently fretted. She should have stayed. She should never have left him. When he strolled out of the shadows a few seconds later, she felt faint with relief.

'You were right,' he drawled cheerfully as he approached the veranda rail and grinned up at her, his teeth gleaming white in the deep tan of his face, his wet black hair slicked back, his hard, muscular body smelling deliciously of the fresh salty sea and the sweet balmy air. 'The surf was great. Absolutely!'

'Humph!' Kelly sniffed indignantly. 'You were gone so long I thought you had surely drowned . . . and I was wondering what I should do with these?' She tossed the bundle down to him. 'You may keep my towel. Goodnight.' With that, she turned smartly on her heel and, with head held high, stepped into her bedroom and closed the door.

Jack grinned at the closed door, tucked the bundle under his arm and, whistling softly, moved with an easy grace through the deep dark shadows of the moonlit night towards the waiting Jeep. Kelly was halfway across her room when she heard his quiet whistle. Her lovely mouth curved gently into an answering smile.

Her man was happy, her heart sang. Her man was safe. She switched off the light just as Jack turned the key in the ignition.

Together they rode under the magic of the moonlit night.

CHAPTER TEN

KELLY was awake long before her alarm clock ordered her up. She had dreamed of Jack and he had proposed to her. Naturally she had accepted and she lay with a smile on her face, thinking about their honeymoon! The sun was just starting to rise over the drifting, turquoise sea, tinting the white, palm-fringed sands a soft pink as she made her way happily across the sleeping compound towards the mess. The fresh morning air had never smelled so sweet. She heard voices coming from the direction of the vans reserved for visiting staff and turned in surprise. Usually no one stirred for at least another fifteen minutes.

Max was holding out a breakfast tray to Amanda Geering. Amanda stood in the doorway, elegantly attired in a black dressing gown fringed with white collar and cuffs, her pale blonde hair blowing in the breeze. Kelly continued along to the mess, thinking her bubbling heart would surely burst. Amanda Geering was in a van of her own! She wasn't sharing with Jack.

Not even the grumblings from the men could dampen her spirits... but it did remind her she had totally forgotten to mention their problem to Jack. She would do so when he came to see her, which would surely be any minute now, she thought happily and filled the enormous sink with water to begin washing the breakfast dishes.

But it was Amanda, not Jack, who paid her the first visit. Amanda stormed in carrying her breakfast tray, looking remarkably cool and elegant in a light beige safari outfit.

'Well!' she snarled, without bothering with any of the usual niceties. 'I can't believe you're still here!'

Kelly's clear green eyes widened in surprise. 'Why wouldn't I be?'

'Why indeed!' Amanda slammed down the tray, making the dishes rattle. 'Jack was absolutely furious with you last night and so was I. I don't take kindly to being bounced around in an opened Jeep while in hot pursuit of a silly little girl!' Her cold blue eyes narrowed meanly. 'He *went* to your dorm. I *assumed* it was to give you your marching papers!'

Kelly's cheeks burned crimson. 'Well, he...he didn't.'

'Obviously!' Her shrewd blue eyes bit into Kelly's face and she added nastily, 'You must do far more for him than simply cook for his employees!'

It was all too much. 'Please get out of my kitchen,' Kelly ordered in a trembling voice as she dried her hands on her apron.

Amanda laughed softly. 'Hit a nerve, have I?' She pointed imperiously to the breakfast tray. 'Max performed the honours this morning but from now on I expect *you* to bring me my breakfast at precisely five o'clock. Two slices of wholemeal bread, lightly toasted, no crusts, a bowl of fresh fruit topped with low-fat yogurt, a pot of piping-hot tea, no milk, just lemon, and on Mondays and Thursdays, a soft-boiled egg. *Soft!*' She added insultingly, 'Can you remember that...or should I write it down?'

Kelly was fuming. 'Better write it down.'

Amanda glared at her. 'Where's some paper and a pen?'

'In that drawer behind you.'

Amanda jotted down her requirements and held out the sheet of paper. 'Here,' she sniped.

Kelly politely took the list, studied it carefully, got out a fresh tray, loaded it with a loaf of wholemeal bread, a bunch of bananas, a ripe golden pawpaw, a few apples, some oranges, a large tub of low-fat yogurt, a half-dozen eggs, studiously checked the list against the contents arranged neatly on the tray, picked it up and handed it to Amanda.

'You will find tea bags, crockery and cutlery in your van. There's also a toaster, kettle, teapot, a small refrigerator and a two-burner stove. I really don't see how you could have overlooked them. They're in plain view.' She smiled at the outrage on Amanda's face and added sweetly, 'Have a nice day!'

Amanda's hands shook as she gripped the tray. 'Jack will hear about this!' she stated venomously.

'I'm sure he will,' Kelly replied cheerfully but her hands were shaking as she lowered them into the dishwater.

Ten minutes later, Jack came into the kitchen. Kelly's heart leapt at the sight of him. He was dressed in work clothes, faded blue jeans and a navy blue T-shirt. He stood looking at her for several heart-wrenching seconds before he spoke.

'How are you feeling this morning?' he asked quietly.

'Fine, thank you,' Kelly answered breathlessly and tucked her fiery mane of hair behind her ears. 'How are you feeling?' she added shyly, her eyes glowing and her voice slightly husky as she stepped closer to him, longing for the feel of his strong arms around her, his lips against her own.

He made no attempt to touch her. 'I heard what passed between you and Amanda!'

'You . . . did?' she asked hesitantly.

'Yes . . . and I wasn't pleased.'

'It's all right,' she lovingly reassured him. 'I can handle Amanda.'

'I wasn't pleased with *you*!'

'*Me*?'

'Amanda is a top architect and several years your senior. How dare you refuse her the small courtesy of preparing her a few simple breakfasts?'

'I didn't! I . . . I mean I wouldn't have . . . had she asked me nicely.'

'Asked you *nicely*!' he exploded. 'Where in blazes do you think you are? This isn't a finishing school. This is a construction camp. And you're the *cook*!'

Kelly stared up at him, hurt flooding her eyes. Did Amanda mean so much to him . . . and herself so little . . . that he could so easily take her part and so readily forget the magic they had shared last night? She felt her heart slowly ripping apart in her chest.

'Are . . . are you saying Amanda has your permission to . . . to push me around? Treat . . . treat me like a s-servant?'

'Of course not! I'm simply saying she has the right to a little bit of respect and I demand that you give that to her. Do I make myself clear?' When Kelly didn't immediately answer, he added harshly, 'Do I?'

'Yes,' she whispered brokenly, her head bowed in anguish.

'You will prepare Amanda's breakfast and take it to her each morning at five o'clock as she requested. Is that understood?'

The pain in her heart leapt to every inch of her body. She forced her head up to look at him, the dreadful hurt lying naked in her eyes. 'No, I...I don't understand.'

'And which part don't you understand?' he ground impatiently.

'The part where I'm suddenly requested to rise at four-thirty when I already work long enough hours as it is...simply to prepare breakfast for someone who has all the facilities in her own van to prepare it for herself. *That's* the part I don't understand!'

Jack dragged a hand wearily across his jaw and around the back of his neck. 'Don't worry, Kelly. I'll see that you're well paid for the extra hours it takes to keep Amanda happy.'

And what about my happiness? her shattered heart cried. She took a deep choking breath to fight the nausea rising in her throat. 'Since...since we're on the subject of extra hours, extra pay, I'm naturally wondering if I will be well paid for the extra hours I spent with *you*? Keeping *you* happy!'

His head snapped back as though she had struck him and for a brief instant Kelly actually thought she saw pain rip through his eyes. But when he spoke, his voice was so cold, so rigidly controlled, she realised she must have imagined it. 'Is that what you want?' he asked icily.

She wanted his love! Tears burned at the backs of her eyes and added to the painful lump in her throat. 'I...I've never made it a secret that...that money has always been my top priority.'

His laugh was bitter. 'That's true. And I haven't for-gotten I promised to pay handsomely for...overtime!' He roughly cupped her chin, his hard fingers biting into her soft skin as he forced her to meet the cold contempt in his eyes. 'And you certainly earned it!' He abruptly released her as though the very sight and feel of her filled him with disgust. Without a further word, he strode out of the kitchen, head held high, powerful shoulders filling up the doorway before he disappeared through it.

Kelly staggered over to a chair and slumped into it, surrendering to her agony. The door slammed and she knew he had shut her out of his life, out of his heart! The tap dripped into the sink, and outside, the water truck lumbered slowly past, spraying the compound. She hunched forward in the chair, her arms folded across her stomach in a futile attempt to ease the pain, as she rocked slowly back and forth, whispering his name, begging his forgiveness, telling him over and over again she hadn't meant those dreadful words.

She finally forced herself out of the chair, stumbled across the kitchen and into the dining room and stood at the screen door, hoping to see him just one more time. The truck was still spraying the compound. Max stood on the veranda of the administration quarters, broom in hand, waiting for it to pass so she could begin her sweeping. Jeeps, loaded with construction workers on their way to the site, and larger vehicles carrying equipment were already carving deep ruts into the wet sand. It was a scene like any other morning, usual in its routine, but to Kelly standing there watching it, nothing would ever be the same again.

Jack stepped out of the administration quarters, his yellow hard hat in his hand. He spoke briefly to Max. Max nodded, quickly leaned the broom against the wall and hurried inside. He raised his dark head and looked across at Kelly standing at the door. Tears streamed down her cheeks and fresh agony filled her heart. He stepped down the stairs and over to a waiting Jeep. With a strangled sob, Kelly burst from the dining room and raced across the compound.

'*Jack*!'

His back stiffened before he slowly turned to watch her run up to him, her hair swirling in a shimmering cloud about her slender shoulders, her face wet with tears. 'Well? What is it?' he demanded coldly.

She winced at his tone. 'I...I haven't told you...haven't told you why I met you at the airstrip.'

'But you have.' His smile was bitter. 'You wanted to make some fast bucks!'

'Please don't!' she pleaded, her eyes filled with torment. 'I don't know what made me say...say what I did. I didn't mean it. Honestly, I didn't.' Her voice broke. 'Last night was so...was so...'

'Profitable?'

'Special!' She added achingly, 'Can't you see...don't you know? *I...I love you, Jack*! *I love you so much*!'

Amanda stepped out of the administration building, a set of rolled-up blueprints in her hands. Kelly dragged her tormented eyes from the harsh, forbidding face of the man she loved and stared blindly down at the hot, dampened sand, certain Amanda had heard her heart-rending confession and witnessed Jack's cold, uncaring reaction.

'See me after work,' Jack issued curtly. 'I'll be here at seven o'clock.'

Kelly nodded and stood back as he slid behind the wheel of the Jeep and leaned across the seat to open the door for Amanda. Amanda tossed her an amused smirk but Kelly didn't care. Jack had told her he would see her tonight and that was the only thing that mattered.

It was the longest day of Kelly's life. She followed her usual routine but her day was plagued, first with hopes, tender and sweet, and then with fears, dark and distressing. One minute she dared hope she had done the right thing by confessing her love; that now he would confess his...for her; that the business with Amanda was simply a silly misunderstanding; that they would laugh over her foolish fears and he would convince her Amanda meant nothing to him.

The next moment she was torturing herself with the possibility that the only reason he had requested her to go to the administration quarters was because it was the official place to fire her! She tried to brace herself to expect and to bravely accept the worse, but no matter how hard she tried, her poor battered heart refused to give up hope.

Once dinner was finally out of the way and the dishes left soaking, Kelly raced across to her dorm and searched for something suitable to wear. But what was suitable? She had no way of knowing. If she wore something romantic, he might think she was taking an awful lot for granted! On the other hand, she didn't want to give the impression she had meekly prepared herself for the gallows!

She finally decided on a compromise. A pale blue skirt and matching sleeveless top with her little white sandals. Attractive without being provocative but still the teeniest bit sexy. She laid the outfit out on her bed along with some fresh undergarments, grabbed a towel, bathrobe, and dashed over to the showers.

At five minutes to seven, Kelly stood in front of her mirror and surveyed the results. Her hair, her eyes, her complexion, all had a special glow like a million candles had been lit inside of her. She was in love and despite her doubts and fears it showed.

A Jeep was parked in front of the administration quarters when Kelly arrived at precisely seven o'clock. The door was shut and she wondered nervously if she should knock. Ordinarily she would walk straight in but that was when Max was there. Max would be in her van now, feet up, enjoying dinner in front of her little portable TV.

Kelly framed her eyes with her hands and peered cautiously through the screen into the semi-darkness. The reception area was deserted but there was a shaft of light beneath the office door at the back. She placed a trembling hand on the knob, opened the door and stepped inside.

It felt so strange being here without Max sitting behind her cluttered desk. Everything was so unnaturally quiet. Kelly strained her ears for any sound coming from behind the closed door. Nothing. She tiptoed quietly over to it, raised her shaking hand and knocked softly.

'Enter!' a deep voice immediately commanded.

Her heart thumped wildly in her chest as she opened the door to the small cubby-hole of an office and stood there like a small frightened doe, too terrified to move. Jack was sitting in a swivel chair facing the door, looking directly at her, a slide-rule in his hands, legs propped up on an old battered desk, feet crossed at the ankles. He held the rule loosely between both index fingers and peered across at her. The light from the desk lamp cast dark, mysterious shadows across his ruggedly handsome features. His hair was still damp from a recent shower and he looked divine in a crisp white silk shirt and caramel-coloured trousers.

'Well?' he growled impatiently. 'Are you going to stand there all night?'

A fierce blush stained her cheeks. He pointed with the slide-rule to a chair directly in front of his desk. Kelly walked stiffly towards it, feeling ridiculously self-conscious, his deep blue eyes making her far too aware of every tingling inch of her body.

The chair was only a few inches from the door but she thought she would never reach it. It seemed as if she was walking in slow motion, but no matter how hard she tried to quicken her steps, her legs refused to go faster. When she did sit down, she carefully avoided his eyes as she crossed her legs and quickly uncrossed them again at the sight of her bare knees. Her heart was pounding so loudly she thought he must surely hear it. She raised a slender hand in a futile effort to still it, but when his eyes followed the movement, it pounded more loudly still. She dropped her hand into her lap and tightly clasped it with the other. Jack shifted slightly in his chair, making it squeak, and this other unexpected sound startled her and she jerked herself upright and a small gasp whispered from her throat.

'Begin!' he commanded.

'Begin?' she repeated shakily.

He waved the slide-rule impatiently in front of him. 'Why you disobeyed orders and came out to the airstrip.'

There was no love, no tenderness in his voice. His whole cold, abrupt manner told her in no uncertain terms what she had feared the whole day. He hadn't invited, no *ordered* her here to talk about her confession, discuss their love, her unwarranted fears about Amanda. How pathetically foolish of her to think he had. He didn't love her. He simply wanted to discuss her problem, get it out of the way so he wouldn't need to deal with her anymore. She had been holding on to a dream and now she felt the dream shattering in her hands.

'For Pete's sake, woman, *talk*!'

'The younger men are getting restless!' Kelly blurted.

A cynical smile twisted his lips. 'I have news for you. So are the older men!'

A deep flush stole across her pale cheeks and she ran her tongue nervously across her lips. 'I...I want to do something about it.'

'And what do you have in mind?' he purred suggestively, his eyes making a bold appraisal of her trembling body.

The flush burst into flames. 'G-Games.'

His black brows shot up. 'Games? Sounds...cosy!'

Tears burned at the backs of her eyes, making them appear unnaturally bright. In desperation she jumped up from her chair. 'Why are you doing this to me?' she begged chokingly and with a stifled sob ran blindly towards the door.

'Don't you *dare* run away!' he bellowed and whipped his legs from off the desk. 'Get back here immediately and finish what you were saying.'

Kelly took a deep steadying breath but it did little to calm her and certainly nothing to alleviate the wrenching pain in her heart. Gathering what was left of her pride, she stiffly made her way back to the chair and perched herself on the edge of it.

'I...I think the boys are missing their families...their friends,' she began in a low, tightly controlled voice. 'They've become bored...restless...'

His black brows furrowed into a frown. 'Have they been giving you trouble?'

'Well, yes, I mean no, well, maybe...just a little.'

Anger flared in his eyes. 'Which is it?'

Despair washed over her. She wanted to help the men, not make things worse for them. Everything was going wrong. *Everything*!

'They're young, high-spirited. They need something to do, something to look forward to in the evenings and on their rostered days off.' She was speaking quickly now, far too quickly, wanting only to make him aware of her observations before she left here, left the camp, left her job, left him! 'I'm...I'm afraid if something isn't done, fights might break out and they could hurt each other or...or cause some other serious trouble, maybe even walk off the job, leave...leave the island,' she finished in a small, sad voice.

'I see.' He frowned and leaned thoughtfully back in his chair, the slide-rule poised in his huge tanned hands, his deep blue eyes intent upon her face as he seriously considered her words. 'What sorts of games did you have in mind?'

'Cricket, softball and beach volleyball for their rostered days off. They could play on the beach. That way they could let off steam, shout and make all the noise they wanted and not disturb the older staff.'

He nodded approvingly. 'And for the evenings?'

'Well, I thought maybe some bingo, Monopoly and Scrabble.'

Amusement glittered in his eyes. 'Bingo?'

She nodded and he chuckled and suddenly she felt herself being lifted from the depths of despair to the dizzying heights of sheer joy. Everything was going to be all right! He liked her plan and approved her suggestions. She could hardly contain herself. She wanted to

jump up from the chair, fling herself into his lap, wrap
her arms around his neck, kiss him, make love to him,
tell him again how much she loved him, needed him . . .

'And I thought, later on, we might even try some one-
act plays,' she continued eagerly, her voice breathless,
her eyes shining as she gazed adoringly across the desk
at him.

'Plays, too? Good gracious!'

His rich warm chuckle tickled the humming strings of
her heart and she leaned forward in her chair, green eyes
sparkling, her rich auburn hair swinging about her
delicate shoulders as she placed her hands on the desk.

'So you approve then? You really do?'

'Indeed, I do! They're great suggestions and certainly
worth trying.' His deep blue eyes held hers. 'Thank you
for taking such initiative. It's a quality I greatly admire
but rarely see nowadays.'

Kelly thought her heart would burst with pride and
happiness at his simple words of praise. He leaned
forward and placed his own hands near hers on the desk.
She ached to touch them, to pick them up and press
them against her cheek, her lips.

'Take the barge across to Airlie Beach tomorrow
morning and get whatever you need,' he continued
warmly. 'Take the whole day,' he added generously. 'You
deserve a break. Max will cover for you and fix you up
with a credit card.'

'Thank you,' she whispered gratefully but she wasn't
thanking him for agreeing to her suggestions or for the
unscheduled break or even for recognizing that she had
worked hard enough to deserve one. She was simply
thanking him for not sending her away.

His eyes held hers as she sat there, gazing across at him, her beautiful, clear green eyes filled to overflowing with the love she felt for him. Suddenly, a cold, hard mask slipped silently over his face and he rose stiffly from his chair. Kelly watched, stunned, as he crossed the small office, opened the door and stood rigidly beside it.

Dismissed! She was being *dismissed*! Now that their meeting was over he obviously couldn't wait to get rid of her. Somehow Kelly managed to pry herself from the chair and make her way across the room. Her frozen body felt his forbidden warmth as she walked woodenly past him. The door banged shut behind her. Her footsteps on the bare floor echoed the terrible bleakness of her heart.

Kelly tossed and turned all that night, hopelessly trapped by the love she felt for this man. She knew she should leave but couldn't. She loved him too much, and sadly, love has no pride. At four-thirty and without having slept, she wearily dragged herself out of bed, washed, dressed, crossed the darkened compound, prepared a tray for Amanda's breakfast and delivered it to her van at five. She told the men before they left for their construction sites that she would be gone for the rest of the day, explained why and that Max would look after them. Max came over a few minutes later with Amanda's breakfast tray, the food untouched. Kelly looked at it, pressed her lips together, but said nothing.

'What's wrong with everybody today?' Max wanted to know. 'You look like something the cat dragged in, Amanda is packing her bag and storming off to Sydney and the Boss is in a raging black mood! I've never seen the likes of it!'

Kelly's heart stood still. 'Amanda is *leaving*?'

'Yup! Thank God!'

'Is…is that why the Boss is in such a…a black mood? Because… because she's *leaving*?'

Max shrugged her shoulders. 'Who knows? All I know is he ordered me over here to relieve you and to give you this for the sports equipment he said you wanted to buy for the lads. By the way, great idea, that.' She handed Kelly a company credit card. 'I'm grateful I won't be over at the administration quarters today,' she sighed. 'Not with the Boss behaving like a grumpy old bear with a thorn stuck in his paw!'

Kelly swallowed the painful lump at the back of her throat. 'It must be because Amanda is leaving. He's…he's m-missing her already,' she added in a small, strained voice. Tears scalded her eyes and she quickly untied her apron and dashed from the kitchen.

Max watched her go and scratched her head. 'Island fever!' she muttered. 'It gets to everyone after a while. Either that, or…!' Her berry brown eyes suddenly sparkled. '*A-ha*!'

CHAPTER ELEVEN

THE barge slipped peacefully through the smooth, crystal-clear waters of the Whitsunday passage. Kelly leaned on the rail and compared Jack's magnificent island to the many others dotting the channel. And while they were all glorious, all spectacular, his, well, his was special. It was special ... simply because it was his!

Sailing ships, luxury yachts, cruisers, catamarans and small fishing fleets added a unique gaiety to the smooth turquoise waters beneath the cloudless sky. The fresh, salty sea breeze whipped Kelly's hair about her face, and by the time the barge pulled up at Shute Harbour, she at least had some colour in her cheeks even if the pain in her heart hadn't lessened. She stepped onto the dock and heard loud voices and laughter behind her. The voices sounded familiar. Too familiar. She whirled around and confronted four grinning faces.

'What are you boys doing here?' she demanded to know. Her eyes darted suspiciously to the barge and back. 'You snuck aboard!'

'It's our rostered day off and we want to help you choose the sporting equipment.'

Kelly didn't believe for an instant they had followed her to the mainland simply to help her choose sporting equipment. She also guessed they hadn't sought permission to come ashore. But she couldn't send them back. There wasn't a barge returning to the island until three o'clock.

'All right,' she reluctantly agreed and added warningly, 'But you're to stay with me the whole time. I don't
want you running off and getting yourselves into any
trouble.'

They boarded a bus for the relatively short drive along
Shute Harbour Road into Airlie Beach, a small coastal
town with fantastic views of the Whitsunday Islands.
Even though it was still an hour from lunch, the boys
insisted they were hungry and wanted to eat before
shopping. Kelly accompanied them into a fast-food
outlet . . . where they somehow managed to disappear!

Annoyed with herself for being so easily and swiftly
duped, Kelly forced herself to remain calm. After all,
she told herself, what mischief could they get into in
such a small town and in broad daylight? She could only
hope they would have the good sense to be at the bus
stop in time for the drive back to the harbour to pick
up the barge at three.

By two o'clock, Kelly had completed her shopping and
had arranged to have the sporting equipment sent over
to the island by barge. She found a small sidewalk café
adjacent to the bus stop, ordered a cappuccino and sat
browsing through a book of amusing one-act plays she
had been lucky enough to find.

But she couldn't concentrate. She was worried about
the young apprentices and felt responsible for them. She
hadn't seen them all day and they weren't at the bus
stop. If they missed the bus, they would miss the barge
and there wasn't another over to the island until the following morning. Jack would be furious.

Her anxiety grew with every passing second. It in-
creased dramatically when the bus pulled up and people
started boarding. Her relief was enormous when she

suddenly spotted the young apprentices making their way haphazardly towards the bus. It vanished altogether when she realised they were *drunk*! Totally! Absolutely!

The driver refused to allow them to board despite Kelly's pleas and promises that she would look after them. The apprentices started arguing and shouting abuse at the driver. A scuffle broke out. Kelly got caught in the middle, trying to break it up. The police were called. The four apprentices, along with Kelly, were hauled off in a paddy wagon to jail, where they were immediately charged and booked. Kelly rang the administration quarters hoping to get Max. But of course Max was over at the mess preparing the evening meal. Jack answered the telephone.

'You're . . . *where*?' he bellowed disbelievingly into the mouthpiece.

He flew immediately over to the mainland in the *Jabiru*. Kelly was taken from a small holding cell and escorted into the reception area by a police officer. Jack stood at the desk, talking to the sergeant, dressed in grey flannels, a crisp white shirt unbuttoned at the neck and a navy blue sports jacket. He turned and looked at her. Kelly quickly lowered her eyes. Having the man she loved seeing her like this, seeing her here, was simply unbearable. She had never felt so disgraced, so ashamed in her entire life.

Her white skirt and yellow shirt were creased and soiled, her hair was mussed, a heel of one white sandal was missing, lost in the fracas. The police officer placed his hand on her elbow and led her up to the desk. She was shivering and felt she had died and gone to hell!

Jack removed his jacket and draped it gently around her shoulders. 'Don't look so frightened,' he said gruffly. 'All charges against you have been dropped.'

'Thank you,' she whispered gratefully and added shakily, 'What about the boys?'

'Their charges remain and they will need to make an appearance later in court, but right now they're on their way back to the island feeling pretty sick and miserable...which is exactly how they deserve to be feeling!' he added harshly.

He placed his arm around Kelly's shoulders and led her outside. She breathed deeply of the clean fresh air. His gleaming silver grey Jaguar convertible was parked at the kerb. She hadn't seen it since they had left Bargara, certainly a century ago!

Jack opened the door and helped her inside. Kelly huddled in the seat and gripped his jacket tightly around her. She couldn't seem to stop shivering. Jack started the powerful motor and turned on the heater despite the warmth of the tropical evening. Neither spoke. When he pulled up to a magnificent mansion high in the hills overlooking the harbour, she assumed he wanted to attend to some business before they drove to the airport. He got out, walked around and opened her door. Kelly stared up at him in alarm, drew back and clutched his jacket even more tightly around her.

'Please don't make me go inside,' she begged. 'Not...not looking like this!'

'This is my home,' he told her quietly and reached for her hand, holding it protectively in his own.

'Your *home*?' Kelly repeated as she allowed herself to be drawn from the soothing darkness of the Jag. *His home*! She had wondered what it would be like, had foolishly dreamed of seeing it someday, having him show it to her, but she had never actually believed it would happen... especially like this.

'I don't relish living full-time in a van,' he told her as he led her up a cobbled stone walkway towards a handsome, solid- looking double oak door. 'When the resort is finished, I'll either sell this or...' He looked intently down at her upturned face and shrugged his massive shoulders. 'Or I'll keep it.'

A manservant, accompanied by a middle-aged maid, opened the door. Kelly was immediately handed over to the maid. She got the distinct impression they had been expecting her. She could only hope they didn't know where she had *been*! She glanced helplessly towards Jack but he was standing in front of an antique hall table in the impressive foyer shuffling through some mail.

'Follow me,' the maid instructed kindly. 'I'll show you to your room.'

'My room?' Kelly repeated, puzzled. 'But...'

Jack turned and frowned at her. 'Do as you're told, Kelly!' He gathered up the correspondence and disappeared down a long, wide, dimly lit corridor, followed by his manservant. Kelly heard a door open and close somewhere in the distance. She turned to the maid, who was watching her with a quiet curiosity. Kelly sighed. There was a feeling of *déjà vu* here.

The maid led Kelly down a corridor in the opposite direction that Jack had gone. She had quick glimpses of huge, lavishly furnished rooms. The atmosphere was one of total quietness, not peace, just a stillness, as if no one actually lived here. She shivered again and clutched the jacket closer around her, grateful no one had taken it from her.

They climbed a wide, gently curving staircase and travelled along another quiet corridor. The carpeting was so thick, their feet made not a whisper of sound. The maid stopped at a door, opened it and stepped inside. Again, Kelly reluctantly followed.

The bedroom was magnificent, enormous, with pale cream-coloured walls, luxurious white carpeting, a king-size bed covered with a pale apricot-coloured satin spread, which exactly matched the drapes lining one whole wall. There was an adjoining bathroom and a private balcony overlooking the magnificence of the Whitsundays. Kelly stood awkwardly in the midst of all this splendour while the maid went into the bathroom and poured her a bath. She handed Kelly a thick blue terry-cloth bathrobe.

'Slip into this and give me your clothes,' she kindly instructed. 'By the time you've bathed and rested, I'll have them returned to you. You will join Mr Saunders for dinner on the terrace at eight.'

Bathed and rested? Dinner with Jack on the terrace? She accepted the robe with trembling fingers, entered the bathroom, removed her clothing and passed them out to the waiting maid. Despite her anxieties, Kelly sank gratefully into the fragrant, rose-scented water, relaxed in it for almost an hour before drying herself with one of the pink, fluffy towels, using the hair-drier, the rich creams and moisturisers obviously laid out for her use and, when she stepped into the bedroom, found that her clothes had already been returned, neatly cleaned and pressed. Even the heel of her sandal had been replaced with a perfect match.

When she had finished dressing and stood in front of the ceiling-to-floor mirror, the sparkle had returned to her eyes. She knew it was because Jack was here, some-where in this deep, silent mansion...and she would soon be joining him for dinner on the terrace!

At five minutes to eight, the maid returned, escorted Kelly to the terrace and discreetly disappeared. Jack was standing with his back to her, facing out to sea. He turned slowly and looked at her. Kelly's heart ham-mered, jumped and wedged tightly in her throat. Never had he looked at her in such a way, as though com-mitting her to memory, *as though this was the last time he would ever see her*!

And then she understood. He had brought her here to say goodbye. Bailing her out of jail had been the last straw. This was to be her farewell dinner. The attentive maid, the beautiful bedroom, the scented bath-water, the creams and moisturisers hadn't been to pamper her as she had so foolishly thought but had merely been part of the farewell package. She had always imagined it would be herself handing in her notice, quitting, leaving him in the lurch. She had even imagined where the scene might take place. But she had never, ever, imagined *this*!

He continued to look at her, his handsome face shrouded in shadows, the moonlight reflected in his eyes, his crisp white shirt in startling contrast with his deeply tanned skin, while Kelly could only stand there, slowly dying, her eyes filled with the worst of all possible agonies.

The breeze blew in from the ocean, lifted her hair, her skirt, fanned her pale cheeks, but she didn't feel it. The same breeze tossed back his coal black hair from his brow and he must have felt it because he moved from the railing and walked slowly over to her, his eyes never leaving her face.

'Are you cold?' he asked and his voice was gruff, gentle, as though he really cared, and she shook her head, no, because she was numb, beyond feeling. He took her hand and led her over to a small round table and she looked down at it and saw how beautifully it had been set, with a white linen tablecloth, sparkling silver cutlery, twinkling crystal goblets and pale pink candles, the tiny flames flickering in the soft tropical breeze.

He's made my farewell dinner very special, she thought and her heart bled. He pulled out a chair, settled her into it, sat down across from her, reached for a bottle of champagne chilling in an antique sterling-silver ice bucket beside the table, filled her glass, then his own. She wondered if he would tell her now that he had decided to terminate her employment or if he would wait until after they had eaten. She picked up her goblet, wrapped her trembling hands tightly around it, took a big gulp, then another. His manservant placed halved avocados, stuffed with king prawns done in a rich creamy sauce, in front of them before silently disappearing into a side entrance.

'I've decided to quit my job!' Kelly blurted, knowing she could never, ever, survive him telling her he didn't want her, didn't need her. 'I won't be returning to the island,' she added quickly, desperately. 'Max can send my belongings to my apartment.'

Jack calmly considered her words and just as calmly speared a prawn with his fork. 'You don't seriously believe I would let you off the hook that easily?' he asked with a growl.

Kelly took another gulp of her champagne. So firing her wasn't punishment enough for daring to fall in love with him and daring to tell him so. He planned to hurt her more. 'Wh-what do you mean?' she stammered shakily.

He looked straight into her eyes. 'You owe me, Kelly McGuire!' he drawled softly.

'Yes, yes, I know. I should have given you at least a week's notice but...but I'm sorry, I...can't.' She bowed her head. 'I just can't!' she added in a tragic little whisper.

'That's not what I meant!'

Something in his voice made her look up quickly. 'What, then?'

'You owe me...for what you've done!'

'What I've done?' Her face went a deathly white and pain rocked her eyes. 'She...she will come back to you.'

Jack frowned. 'She?'

'Amanda,' Kelly whispered.

The frown deepened. 'Why are we talking about Amanda?'

'Don't...don't you want to?'

'Hell, no!'

Kelly's eyes widened. 'But...but you *love* her!'

He laughed. 'You've got to be joking! Amanda would have to be the most unlovable creature this side of the Pacific.'

Kelly could hardly believe her ears. 'But...but Max said you were in a raging black mood this morning because...because she was leaving and...'

'I was upset all right but it had nothing to do with Amanda's leaving. Why would it when I sacked her?'

'You *sacked* her?'

'It was a long time in coming. Amanda has always been difficult to get along with but lately she has become much worse, pushing her weight around and constantly, despite several warnings, upsetting staff. She might be a great architect but unfortunately she's sadly lacking in people skills. I told her to leave the moment she finished complaining about the breakfast you served her!' He picked up his goblet and leaned comfortably back in his chair. 'Now, shall we get back to why you owe me?'

Kelly was stunned. He didn't love Amanda. *He didn't love Amanda*! Soft, romantic music spilled from speakers onto the terrace. It perfectly matched the music in her heart. 'Well...well, you gave me a job when no one else would. I...I owe you for that.'

Jack raised his glass to his lips and gazed at her over the brim. 'It's not that. It's...something else,' he drawled mysteriously, his dark eyes gleaming, looking at her as though she should *know*!

Kelly shook her head, tears suddenly springing to her eyes. She owed him so much. Thanks to him she still had her apartment and money in the bank to keep her until she found another job. 'You...you rescued me from jail,' she said in a small, choking voice. 'And...and kept my name out of the record books.'

He rose from his chair, walked around the table and touched a tear rolling down her cheek. 'You made me fall in love with you!' he whispered huskily.

She stared up at him. 'I *did*?'

'Most definitely.'

'You're in *love* with me?'

'Totally!' His smile was tender as he drew her to her feet, lovingly cupped her face in his huge hands and this time there was no mask to hide from her his true feelings. It was there in his eyes for her to plainly see and she heard it in his voice as he passionately spoke.

'I think I've loved you since we did that interview at Bargara. I know I was certainly intrigued with you even before we'd met, when I was constantly reading what you were saying about me to the newspapers.' Amusement glittered in his eyes as he continued to gaze adoringly down at her, as though he could never get enough of her. 'I couldn't believe your nerve, your audacity. When you drove up in that battered old truck and looked up at me with those big, beautiful green eyes, so full of fight and fire, well, my darling, all I wanted was to drag you off then and there, and—' he bent his dark head and kissed her tenderly on the lips '—make you mine!'

'Oh, Jack!' she breathed, her eyes shining through her tears. 'I . . . I've waited so long to hear you say that!'

He stroked her hair back from her face. 'I would have said it sooner, but . . .' A fierce, proud light burned in his eyes. 'But until this morning, I thought it was only the money keeping you on the island! And it hurt like hell!'

Pain filled her eyes. 'I only made you believe that to protect myself, to protect my heart! That . . . that night when I waited up for you, I smelled perfume on your jacket and . . . and . . . I was so hurt, so jealous . . . but I didn't realize how much or how deeply I loved you until I met you at the airstrip and then . . . and then when I smelled the same perfume on Amanda, I . . . I wanted to *die*!'

He shook his head and gently traced the curve of her cheek. 'If only you had said something, had asked me.'

'I . . . I was afraid,' she whispered hoarsely.

He took her hand and led her over to the edge of the terrace. There was a wooden bench facing out towards the harbour. He sat down and pulled her onto his lap. 'From this minute forward,' he said quietly, holding her close, 'I want you to trust me enough to ask me, tell me, or show me anything you wish and I promise to do the same with you. I don't want either of us to ever suffer needlessly this way again. Do you promise me, Kelly?'

'I promise you,' she whispered fervently.

'Good!' His arms tightened around her as he sighed his satisfaction.

Kelly pulled slightly away from him so she could clearly see his face. 'How *did* that perfume get on your jacket?'

His rich, warm chuckle washed over her. 'Amanda was one of the architects at our dinner meeting. She took her perfume from her purse, opened it and managed to spill it. I gave her my handkerchief to mop it up and afterwards put it back in my pocket.' He pulled her close. 'Now, don't you feel just a little bit foolish?' he murmured teasingly against her lips.

Kelly was silent. Jack crooked a finger under her chin, gently forcing her to look up at him. 'You're wondering why I didn't say I loved you this morning,' he murmured softly.

Kelly nodded, a lump forming at the back of her throat from the remembered pain. 'You were so c-cold and... and stiff... and I thought...'

'I know!' His eyes filled with agony at the hurt he saw in her own. 'I wanted desperately to believe you but your eyes were the colour of moss and...'

'You thought I was lying?' A cry tore from her throat. 'Oh, Jack, I was breaking up inside!'

'We both were!' He framed her face with his hands, looking deeply into her eyes. 'I love you, Kelly,' he cried hoarsely. 'You are the woman I've been searching for but never hoped to find. You're my life, my joy, my fun. You're my everything!'

Her heart spun at the love she saw burning in his eyes. She wrapped her arms around him, her cheek against his chest, and listened to the powerful thumping of his heart.

'When you didn't return on that barge I almost went crazy thinking something terrible had happened to you.' A shudder ripped through his body. 'I was getting ready to search for you when you rang. I don't ever want to go through that again. I want you by my side forever, Kelly. I love you and I want you to marry me.' He held her at arm's length and added warningly, 'I won't take no for an answer!'

'And I wouldn't let you! Oh, Jack! I love you so much it...it hurts!'

Her heart continued to spin. She thought it would burst with happiness. He loved her! He had loved her all along! She drew his face down and kissed him with all the love and passion and hunger that surged from her heart.

'The smartest thing I ever did,' he murmured huskily against her lips, 'was hiring you!'

Kelly smiled. She had waited a long time to hear that! He stood up, took her hand, led her across the terrace and down a set of steps. Fairy lights lit up the path as they strolled through the shadowed grounds. 'Do you remember I promised to listen to some of your gardening ideas after you finished your cooking contract?'

'I remember.'

'Well, this is our garden.' He smiled lovingly down at her starlit eyes. 'And I'm listening!'

MILLS & BOON

By Request

Bestselling romances brought back to you by popular demand

Two complete novels in one volume
by bestselling author

Roberta Leigh

Two-Timing Man

◆

Bachelor at Heart

Available: March 1996   Price: £4.50

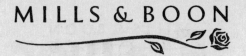

MILLS & BOON

Next Month's Romances

Each month you can choose from a wide variety of romance with Mills & Boon. Below are the new titles to look out for next month.

CLIMAX OF PASSION	Emma Darcy
MARRYING MARY	Betty Neels
EARTHBOUND ANGEL	Catherine George
A WEEKEND TO REMEMBER	Miranda Lee
HOLLYWOOD WEDDING	Sandra Marton
COMING HOME	Patricia Wilson
A CAREFUL WIFE	Lindsay Armstrong
FAST AND LOOSE	Elizabeth Oldfield
CHARLOTTE'S COWBOY	Jeanne Allan
SISTER OF THE BRIDE	Valerie Parv
ONE-NIGHT WIFE	Day Leclaire
HEARTLESS STRANGER	Elizabeth Duke
DANGEROUS GROUND	Alison Kelly
TENDER CAPTIVE	Rosemary Carter
BRIDE OF MY HEART	Rebecca Winters
TOO LATE FOR REGRETS	Liza Hadley

Available from WH Smith, John Menzies, Volume One, Forbuoys, Martins, Woolworths, Tesco, Asda, Safeway and other paperback stockists.

Fl✿wer P✿wer

How would you like to win a year's supply of simply irresistible romances? Well, you can and they're free! Simply unscramble the words below and send the completed puzzle to us by 31st August 1996. The first 5 correct entries picked after the closing date will win a years supply of Temptation novels (four books every month—worth over £100).

1	LTIUP	TULIP
2	FIDLADFO	
3	ERSO	
4	AHTNYHCI	
5	GIBANOE	
6	NEAPUTI	
7	YDSIA	
8	SIIR	
9	NNAIATCRO	
10	LDIAAH	
11	RRSEOIMP	
12	LEGXFOOV	
13	OYPPP	
14	LZEAAA	
15	COIRDH	

Please turn over for details of how to enter 🖘

Hw t enter

Listed overleaf are 15 jumbled-up names of flowers. All you have to do is unscramble the names and write your answer in the space provided. We've done the first one for you!

When you have found all the words, don't forget to fill in your name and address in the space provided below and pop this page into an envelope (you don't need a stamp) and post it today. Hurry—competition ends 31st August 1996.

Mills & Boon Flower Puzzle
FREEPOST
Croydon
Surrey
CR9 3WZ

Are you a Reader Service Subscriber?   Yes ☐   No ☐

Ms/Mrs/Miss/Mr _____

Address _____

_____

_____ Postcode _____

One application per household.

COMP396
B